Sebastiano's Vine

Sebastiano's Vine

Carmelo Militano

Ekstasis Editions

© 2013 Carmelo Militano
Second Printing 2022
Cover image: *Bacchanals*, 1891, plaster relief by French sculptor Aimé-Jules Dalou

Published in 2013 by:

Ekstasis Editions Canada Ltd.   Ekstasis Editions
Box 8474, Main Postal Outlet   Box 571
Victoria, B.C. V8W 3S1   Banff, Alberta T1L 1E3

LIBRARY AND ARCHIVES CANADA CATALOGUING IN PUBLICATION

Canada Council   Conseil des Arts
for the Arts   du Canada

Ekstasis Editions acknowledges financial support for the publication of *Sebastiano's Vine* from the government of Canada through the Canada Council for the Arts.

Printed and bound in Canada.

*To the memory of Domenico Militano
and Carmela Foti.*

For Vera, Adrianna, Tony, Rosa, and Pina.

There is no end. There is no beginning.
There is only the infinite passion of life.

~ Federico Fellini

We are fragments of an unutterable whole.

~ Charles Simic

Why this story?

Maybe it was the white winter nothingness of Winnipeg. Maybe it was my backhand script, slanted left as if bent by the wind. Maybe it was my spelling: the mixing of *i* and *e* (the 'I' in my heart conflicted with the 'eye' in my head). Maybe it was my wanting to be liked by everyone: the perfect Canadian, the perfect child. Maybe it was about fear. Maybe it was my rejection of the Canadian Prairies' writing model with its feints and false modesty, its hidden clubbiness, its embrace of radical literary theory born on the gilded streets of the Left Bank and its tourist cafes, its crossed leg over knee poet pose; the Anglican tweedy gentleman with pipe model rejected and replaced with the taciturn, faded-denim-jacket-and-jeans farmer model, overwhelmed by the immensities of sky, prairie, and ruthless weather. Maybe it was about being raised in the middle of the continent and always on the verge of disappearing. Maybe the story began when my Italian great-grandfather lay his thick fingers on the table and listened to the Lupino family's accusations. Maybe it was the wine and the land that produced it. I don't have an answer. All I know is that the story had to be told. So I sat down two summers ago…

I was born on the second floor of a stone cottage perched at the edge of a small Calabrian village, above my grandfather's ancient farming tools and a row of stout wine barrels belted with black strips of rusting tin.

The day was hot and my grandfather was in his garden when a villager came running and announced my birth. Dropping his *zappa*, a short-handled hoe, my grandfather spread his arms wide and shouted to the grey-green olive leaves above. It is uncertain whether God heard his words of thanks.

~~~

My ancestors opened the red earth around ancient olive trees, weeding out stray bits of wild oat and barley so the roots could breathe. They broke the soil with slow, steady slaps of their zappas, the rhythm and sound of metal against the earth like the hip-to-hip smack of Lucia and I. Sweat beaded their brows (as it did on mine), stained their thin wool shirts, trickled down their backs, and finally rested on the rim of their trousers.

Their peasant lot was forever, and trying to find their beginning was like trying to find the origins of time. What is certain is that they (and I) came from a long line of *con-tandini*, peasant farmers, stretching back to the eternal olive trees, to the time when there was finally peace with Persia, and the ancient Greek playwright Euripides staged his first play.

~~~

—You-rippa-deez panties? Ha ha, very funny. Good fake Italian accent, Michael, she said after. I was lying next to her, still breathing hard into her ear, my arm across her stomach, smiling at my own pun.

—But I did. Sorry. I know your nosy aunt will figure it out if they go missing. I'm only thinking of you.

—You are such a good boy, Michael. But you don't fool me. Don't worry about my aunt or me.

She tossed her torn underwear towards the riverbank. The spring runoff would rise and carry them away, just as our desires had carried us away that afternoon, from the narrow world and expectations of Italian family life.

Where did this family begin, you ask?

~~~

What is known is that my family began with Sebastiano Filo, my grandfather. The year, day, and month he was born is uncertain. His height, shoulders, and last name carried the traces of an ancient Greek past and, like the ancient Greeks, a deep suspicion of foreigners. His gift was the ability to graft with perfection and care any grapevine in the region. He tended the vineyards of the wealthy landowners, and was known locally as *Il Medico,* the doctor, whenever a vine needed mending or perhaps an owner wished to change the grape variety in his vineyard.

On the other side of our family tree is a silent noticer, a man who always watched and spoke *poche parole*, few words. The watcher in him is where the writer in me began.

This was my maternal grandfather. His name was Carmine Maldenti; his moustache full, his eyes steady (like those of a tax collector, it was said). He sat firm and remote, his thick fingers flat on a wooden table hidden inside one of the many caves burrowed into the side of the mountain known as Aspromonte, listening to the affronted Lupino clan. He was known locally as *Il mastero*, the master, and was both feared and respected. His word was final.

The Maldenti family he headed was sly, ceremonial, and honour-bound—a gossip-mongering, competitive, loud, loyal, and treacherous bunch; the men hard, the women stubborn. In other words, a proud family.

Is it possible it all began here in this remote patch of Calabria that few knew about or cared to know, where the long arm of the state never quite reached, where custom and fear always outdistanced the remote penal codes decreed in Rome?

October 1963

I saw Lucia for the first time at the steps of Somerset School. It was a cold morning and her breath rose and disappeared in front of her pretty face. Teachers were lining us up in rows to enter the school: boys in one line, girls in another. I noticed how she laughed and shook her hair and stamped her feet to keep warm.

Later I found out she lived on Sherbrook, a busy one-way street that brought doctors, nurses, and medical students from the shady lawns and boulevards of Wellington Crescent and River Heights to the grime and dust of the West End.

Squeezed between the Rehab Centre and the General Hospital sat Holy Rosary Church. I sat in the balcony on Sunday morning and watched eleven-thirty Mass. I had gone to Mass with dread, and also the vague hope of seeing Lucia. I had no idea what I was supposed to do or say if I did.

We sat, kneeled, and stood according to the rhythms and rituals of the service. We said 'Amen' and 'the Lord be with you' at the right times; bowed our heads when the bells chimed and when Father Moro lifted up the Eucharist like a victory cup.

At the back of the church, blue, red and white votive candles flickered in front of a large statue of Mary. In her arms was her dead son, horrible purple and red wounds all over his body. At the front of the church was the altar. On each side, statues of saints in sackcloth expressed colourless contentment. Small gilded angels gestured for us to look upward at the cross, bright and bursting with golden rays.

Lucia arrived for Mass dressed in her Sunday best. She wore a navy-blue coat over a frilly white dress that peeked past the coat's hem. Grey wool socks were pulled up to her knees, and her black leather shoes shone like a waxed floor. A bright shiny hair band held back her dense, curly hair.

Mass ended and parishioners slowly made their way down the aisles, smiling and nodding to each other. The crowd spilled onto the church steps. Women, children-in-hand, stopped briefly to talk. The men lingered on the sidewalk, in groups of three or four, and smoked and talked while the women and children scattered home.

Lucia and her aunt were halfway down the street before I exited the church. It was a relief when they disappeared without knowing I had been watching them from the balcony.

~~~

Lucia sat at the front of the class with the rest of the girls. When she smiled, her bright blue-grey eyes flashed like sunlight on chrome. I sat as far as possible from the front, and Mrs. Price's desk.

At the back of the classroom I doodled, sketching fish beneath a wavy, watery bunch of lines and small boats on top. Boats were easy to draw: strike a line at an angle for the bow, connect two parallel lines from the bow with another straight line, add a few round portals, and presto, you had a boat. I wasn't much of an artist. I wasn't much of a student. Some of my classmates thought I was dumb.

Mrs. Price talked and talked.

The room was stuffy and hot. Our coats and scarves hung on black cast-iron hooks at the back of the room. Melted snow pooled beneath our winter boots and stained the hardwood floor.

The rusty old radiators under the big windows hissed, and then clanked as if struck by a wrench.

The hardwood floors outside the classroom creaked as someone walked by.

A sparrow flew past the window.

The sky was grey. The schoolyard trees were bare.

Mrs. Price stopped, at last.

—That will be all for today. Lunchtime.

She dismissed us, row by row, to get on our coats and boots.

I came flying out of the building, happy to be finally released. Lucia was standing at the school gate near the flagpole, waiting.

—Judy asked me to invite you to her birthday party.

—Why doesn't Judy ask me herself?

—I'm her best friend and I'm helping her. So are you coming? It will be a lot of fun.

—Will you be there?

—Of course, silly. I'm helping her, remember? And I am her best friend.

She turned and ran down the street towards the traffic lights at the corner of Notre Dame and Sherbrook. It started to snow, so I took off in the opposite direction towards Payfair's brown-and-white awning, to wait out the snow. I stood and watched the big soft flakes hit the asphalt. Cars swished by, windshield wipers flapping back and forth.

I was thrilled but felt exposed somehow. Did Lucia know I liked her? Judy and I did shout at each other in the schoolyard at recess, and once me and another boy played hopscotch with Lucia and Judy. What had I done to let her know? Well, at least she would be there without the watchful eye of her aunt or her angry father. I wondered what she had said to escape her family.

The snow stopped. I wanted to get home and have something to eat. It was March and the tight green buds on the trees had yet to open. The arms of the trees stretched upward, seeking the neck of the sky. I walked down Furby Street past the Molson Breweries, happy and excited. It was the first time Lucia and I had spoken to each other.

April 1993

The ancient Acropolis stood noble, bright, and aloof in the moonlight like a broken, beautiful white mansion.

Lucia adjusted her hips and sighed for so much beauty. I took an ice cube and ran it across her shoulders. The water drops streaked down her back and pooled on the dent above her cheeks. It reminded me of the way water had pooled by our winter boots in elementary school.

Blue cigarette smoke curled upward and hung in the room. We lay silent, as we once had underneath the old elms by the river near the Cornish Library, the same river Hughie had dropped into so long ago, only to reappear months later near the Lockport dam, bloated and disfigured.

The next morning we headed out towards a café she liked near Omnia Square. She wore a loose-fitting white shirt that caught the gentle curve of her breasts. Her curly hair fell like a dark waterfall and her blue-grey eyes were mischievous and alert. She was happy.

I noticed how her face blended naturally with the faces on the streets. She could have been any one of the Minoan women in ritual procession on the frescoed walls at the ancient palace of Knossos: long dark hair, aquiline nose, large kohl-lined eyes, subtle curved smile.

We found the café in a bowl of white light at the end of a side street. Under the shade of a dusty blue-striped canopy, a few Greek men flapped worry beads. As we entered the café, another group of men, drinking coffee and smoking, stared at us.

It was our second morning in Athens. Two months earlier she had phoned to ask me to meet her there; her therapist had told her it would be good for her to make peace with her past and she had finally gotten up the nerve to call.

—I know it's short notice and you probably still hate me, but Michael, say yes.

—Lucia. It was a long time ago.

Her tone and approach was not all that different from how she had invited me, years before, to Judy's birthday party. A few facts and not much by way of obvious emotion. Casual and conspiratorial, yet at the same time she was asking for my help. I knew that her bland, cool demeanor was her way of appearing to be in control. It was a habit she had picked up long ago from living in a household where the slightest misplaced word would cause her father's rage to erupt. It was also her way of protecting herself from thinking too hard about the past—though it was impossible not to remember it, even if only in fragmented bits (like this story), vague as to how the pieces would fit together.

Childhood is the garden where the future adult is created. Is that what she was doing? Revisiting her past? Is it possible to put the apple back on the tree?

But a part of me—a part I didn't want to admit to—still wanted to see her, despite all that had happened so long ago.

—Okay Lucia, I'll meet you in Athens.

—Michael, I never stopped thinking about you.

—Thanks. Same. Lucia…

—Yes, Michael?

—Nothing. I'll tell you when I see you.

—Oh, if you could see me now! I have a smile from ear to ear.

What I had wanted to say was that I was still angry. She had returned and stirred up all the old emotions. I thought

I was a fool to agree to see her again but I felt compelled. I wanted to return to the garden.

December 1963

Hughie Murphy lived halfway down Langside Street in an old side-by-side with a broken veranda. The wooden steps were unpainted and slippery, the handrail as unsteady as a midnight drunk. The backyard was mainly dried-up dirt without a shred of grass anywhere, the exact opposite of an Italian garden. It was a dump, littered with pork-and-beans tins, plastic wrap, dried-up chicken bones, and rusted, foul-smelling garbage cans. The remains of last month's Saturday comic pages bled pink and blue against a corner fencepost. A decrepit green couch covered in black moldy spots, its coiled springs exposed, lay rotting against the tottery wood fence.

Hughie lived with his mother and father, an uncle, and his older brother Brian. I never saw any of them except his brother. Brian's face was always marked with a purple, black, or yellow-green bruise; his knuckles raw and scratched red. He fought in a parking lot across the street from Somerset School. Brian was a dirty, cruel fighter. At some point in a fight, especially if it was not going his way, he would slip on brass knuckles. He was merciless, punching and kicking his victims to the ground. Someone always had to call the cops, out of fear and mercy for the other guy, and Brian usually ended up in the back of a cruiser.

The inside of Hughie's house was also a disaster. Dirty dishes were piled up in the kitchen sink; empty pop bottles and long-necked beer bottles lay defeated all over the house. Overflowing ashtrays sat on either side of a battered brown couch. The air was thick with the smell of burnt toast. I avoided going into his house, even on cold winter days. The burnt/sour smell was overwhelming.

I stood on the edge of the veranda and waited, worried that someone might see me hanging around the worst household in the neighborhood and tell my parents. Hughie appeared, wearing a brown, water-stained winter coat and a black knit cap with a moth hole on the side, pulled down low. We took off down the street towards the Molson's parking lot to defend a snow mountain made overnight by front-end loaders.

Hughie's family ignored him, but he didn't seem to mind. He'd eat whenever he wanted, and whatever he wanted. His favourite foods were hotdogs and jam busters. He ate wieners year-round, raw or cooked, with or without a bun, and usually with a Coke or 7UP. He'd finish off his meal with a chocolate bar or doughnut.

He stayed out late and wandered around downtown when it pleased him, and made friends with street people and teenage crooks. His life was different from that of the rest of us at school. We were bogged down with supper hours and mothers who insisted we eat a hot lunch. There was no other language in his house as there was in mine, where Italian (or more specifically, the Calabrian dialect) was spoken, which I slipped into unconsciously the minute I walked over the doorsill and greeted my mother.

At Hughie's place there was no one in the kitchen stirring a pot, slicing a vegetable or peeling a potato, or sitting at a Singer machine, sewing zippers onto winter jackets that

Maurice, the factory manager, brought over every Thursday—piecework to earn extra money: what my mother and aunt in their Italian /English patois called *cocuito e jacki*, sewing jackets.

Hughie's messy home was loose and easy, like a pair of old summer shorts. My home was full of food, work, duty; a tug-of-war between English and Italian, between sleep and play, between summer light and winter dark, between order and chaos, madness and sanity, sickness and health. I envied his freedom. It was in the air. It was in the music. It was somehow in my youthful blood, and I longed to get away from the customs and rules of my newly minted immigrant family and slip into an unencumbered life full of adventure. Instead there was my sad mother and demanding father, and the harness of tradition and the weight of a social code born and bred in the far distant mountain villages of Calabria.

My father had left Calabria for Canada shortly after it was certain my mother was pregnant, to spike rail in blistering summer heat, and to sweep snow from switches when the winter winds blew harsh and relentless. I was four by the time my mother and her sister made the trip across the Atlantic. (The dolphins followed the ship, she said. My mother and aunt cried every day, staring at the wide Atlantic.)

Southern Italy lived as a kind of Shangri-la in my mother's mind, full of sunshine and fresh air, where the predictable rhythms of the seasons, the soft clatter of evening dinner dishes, the loud Thursday market days, and the still and silent holy days each fell one after the other, bringing comfort, laughter, and security to what was essentially a dangerous and unpredictable world. In Canada, her worry and sadness deepened during the long, cold winter months when storms arrived full of wind and snow, and she was left alone worrying and waiting for my father to return from his job at the Fort Rouge rail yard. What would she do if he did not come home? Who would help her? Where would she find money to live, or to return to her family? Who would understand her bad English?

I lay in bed listening to the wind howl, its sudden bursts drowning out the quiet sobs of my mother in her room across the narrow hallway.

April 1993

The bus left Athens in the early afternoon for Delphi. Lucia and I sat near the back.

We travelled on a narrow highway below the ancient city of Thebes. In the distance were the shadows of mountains across the plains. The smooth black asphalt twisted and turned up into the mountains where thin ewes and their lambs scattered alongside the road, not a shepherd in sight. The light was weak in the sky and fell in pale white streaks through the assembled armada of clouds. This was an ancient land with ancient ghosts, curiously serene and silent and absent of people. I thought it mirrored our situation, minus the antiquity.

I was looking for a starting point, a dawn of sorts, a beginning and an end, an explanation of what had happened to Lucia. To us.

We arrived at Delphi in the middle of the afternoon and found a tiny taverna about a hundred metres from the small bus depot. Next door was a whitewashed building with the word HOTEL painted in black. Behind it, a garden with fig and orange trees in large red clay pots bordered a scattering of café tables shaded by umbrellas. In the distance, a road ran towards the low, dark mountains and then vanished behind in a quick curve like an embrace.

After three days of Athenian noise and traffic, the small hotel and garden were a welcome counterpoint. We ate a lunch of tomato salad with bits of blue onion in a dense, green olive oil; stuffed eggplants; and thick white bread, washed down with retsina. The food reminded us of meals we used to have at home as children…but Lucia didn't want to talk about those times.

Afterwards, we walked up the street to another café for coffee. I tried again to bring up the past. She walked with her shoulders slumped, smoking, and brushed back her curly hair from her face with her free hand.

—I'm sorry, Michael. I thought this trip would help us…or at least, me. I guess I was wrong. I'm so exhausted. It was all so long ago and pointless. Do you see what I mean?

Her mood had changed after our first nights together in Athens. I still wanted to know what had happened between her and Hughie when we were teenagers. I wanted her to see and understand my old anger and resentment. But the moment it bubbled to the surface she stopped talking. This added to my frustration.

—For Chrissake, Lucia, stop being so selfish. You asked me to be here with you.

—I don't know what I want anymore. Maybe just to live and grow old, drying slowly like a leaf.

I said nothing. I interpreted her not knowing as a form of self-indulgence and protection. We returned in silence to the hotel, and fell asleep with our arms and legs wrapped around each other. But the past lay between us, like an invisible river inside a dark, steep canyon.

~~~

The Second World War had cast a long shadow that changed Lucia's father's life forever, one early morning in Northern Greece. I knew that further north of Delphi and to the west was where Domenico had been wounded. His Italian platoon, stationed in the northwestern corner of Greece, had been advancing on a muddy mountain road in the cold Pindus Mountains, near the unmarked Albanian border. The lower slope of the Pindus was thick with pine and skinny birch saplings. Under the trees, wild prickly bushes spread out across the forest floor in an irregular undergrowth of savage green. Perfect setting for an ambush.

It was a damp, cold day. First snow, then freezing rain, then death, quick and brief.

The buzz of bullets and thud of mortars sprayed chunks of mud and stone everywhere. The Italian soldiers scattered off the road in a vain attempt to find cover. They never managed to fire a shot. Most fell dead with wounds large as grapefruits.

An eerie silence fell, like the one after a horrible car accident, except for the screams of the wounded and the moans of the dying. Shot in both legs and with bits of shrapnel in his head, Domenico managed to roll off the edge of the road into the thick undergrowth

~~~

The next day we visited the ruins that spread up the side of Mount Parnassus. We explored the Stoa first, the great hall built by the Athenians to house war trophies after their victory over the Persians. The tender early-morning light added to its elegiac feel, and the mood of the place seemed to match our heavy hearts. We continued up the sacred path to the theatre carved into the lower side of the mountain, and stopped to take in the view. Pines and cypresses formed an irregular series of small V-shaped ridges and ravines that dropped into a long, narrow valley. To our right was a blue strip of water, the Gulf of Corinth, mist floating above it like a white muslin veil. Directly below, five weathered Doric columns, the remains of the temple of Apollo, glowed a faint gold and red.

We walked further up the path and arrived at the stadium, a long oval-shaped arena with rows of ancient stone seats. Tufts of grass grew between the cracks.

The entire holy site stood empty and silent under an immaculate, polished blue sky. It was as if we had fallen into a melancholy dream with our eyes open. The ruins, awe-inspiring, felt like defeat.

Lucia found the narrow cave of the ancient oracle of Delphi. It was one of the reasons we were here. Lucia pressed her cheek against the water-stained wall. Her soft voice caressed the stone like a painter's brush. She whispered about how Greece had damaged her father, of his permanent anger, of years lost in unexplainable grief. And she asked to be forgiven—was it not enough that she was barren?

She received no answer from the oracle, no cryptic message from the gods; just the rhythmic trickle of water, measuring time.

July 1966

Hughie, Lucia, and I were friends. Hot July afternoons found us splashing and falling in the pool at Notre Dame Park— our towels never dry, we were in and out the water so often. Afterwards, we'd usually stop to see the turtles for sale in Woolworth's, then the goldfish and lizards in the aquariums at the back of Mike's Pet Store on Sargent. When we emerged, blind for a second, into the bright sunlight, our fingers smelled of slime from touching the back of an exotic fish when old Mike was busy with a customer.

Sometimes we headed downtown to visit the wonders in Eaton's. The top floor was a maze of expensive furniture: model living room and dining room suites, kitchenettes, lamps, wall clocks, and the latest colour TVs. We'd sit in the leather armchairs, imagining ourselves to be wealthy home-owners, until one of the salesclerks in a tie and jacket, hands gesturing in disapproval, shooed us away like houseflies. Our next stop was the bedroom displays, where we'd lay on the mattresses, commenting on how soft or hard they felt. But we were quick about it, ever wary of the sales staff.

We'd then move on to the basement. Here was the candy department, the counter stacked with Swiss and German chocolate bars; O'Henry, Jersey Milk and Cadbury bars; lemon drops, toffee, mints, and gumdrops. Below the counters were plastic bins full of small chunks of peanut brittle and an assortment of candies wrapped in shiny gold, green, or blue paper. We'd glanced over our shoulders like jewellery thieves before slyly picking up a candy or two from the open bins, then head directly for the stairs and out the door, our mouths full.

At the corner of Donald and Portage, a short, fat man with an unlit cigarette hanging from his bottom lip sold newspapers he held down with a brown brick, out of a rusty wagon. Hughie was always up for trying to steal a newspaper off his cart. He rarely succeeded.

One weekend afternoon, Portage Avenue was alive with cars and big electric buses, their trolley poles now and again popping off blue sparks. Heat rose in waves off the sidewalk. Elderly women tottered about, pulling small shopping carts. Groups of giggling teenage girls sauntered by, clutching blue-and-white shopping bags. Scruff-looking guys in jean jackets and greasy hair loitered at street corners, drawing on cigarettes. Old men sporting summer fedoras waited at bus stops. A few street people passed us, faces blank and dazed. Behind shop windows, mannequins—heads and noses tilted upwards—stared down on us.

At the Bay, we cut through the women's perfume section, the many scents ricocheting off our nostrils as we headed to the Malt Shop in the basement. It was a Saturday afternoon, so the place was packed with teenagers, young couples, and women of all ages out shopping. There were no free tables, so we stood at a counter ledge, sharing a malt, watching the waitresses in their black fishnet stockings dart between tables with trays of grilled cheese sandwiches, hamburgers, pies, coffees, Cokes and fries.

The room was alive with the buzz of people and the clatter of plates, forks and spoons. A cloud of blue tobacco smoke hung overhead. It looked like a wealthy and sophisticated kingdom, beyond our adolescent reach, and we wanted to be a part of it. I felt my secret, erotic self yearn each time a waitress passed by. Desire made no sense to me;

its brief intensity shocking. They looked mature and unapproachable, and my feelings seemed farfetched and whimsical. The only sensible way to deal with my desire was to ignore it. Hughie, on the other hand, was delighted. Do you see the ass on that girl? he whispered.

I looked, and then turned away. Lucia smiled without parting her lips, the same smile I saw years later on the streets of Athens, the same smile I would see in the grain elevator later that summer. The feelings under our skin were new, and although none of us were prepared to say it, exciting.

I imagined my world transformed and better, once I knew the secret, but for now I felt embarrassed by the concealed fruit that revealed itself at every turn: bright red lips across the aisle on a bus, a pair of long legs on the beach, a brassiere hanging on a laundry line. I was in awe of the women who created this desire: their beautiful curves, soft indulgent smiles and easy laughter, the twinkle in their eyes that seemed to imply they knew more than I could ever know and it was useless trying to divine what they were thinking. They guarded the key to a secret world, hidden and erotic. How did one enter that garden without stepping on the flowers? It was all so mysterious, thrilling, and scary.

I am from Southern Italy. Calabria, to be specific: the mythical and magical toe about to boot Sicily. Legend has it that it was along western Calabria's coastline that Morgan le Fay, the half-sister of King Arthur and apprentice to Merlin, advised Roger the Second, the Norman king, how to invade Sicily in the eleventh century. Morgan le Fay, of course, was a witch and famous for her local spell and legend.

The Fata Morgana spell occurs when, by chance, the right humidity, limpid air, a certain mathematical angle of the sun's rays, and a thin white cloud cover, all come together; and waiters, fruit peddlers, fishermen, sailors, lawyers, bankers, masons, doctors, housewives, prostitutes, students—in short, all the people of Messina going about their daily business at the edge of the city appear to float in the Strait of Messina. For those along the Calabrian coast gazing out to sea, for one brief shiny moment or two, the city of Messina shimmers on top of small rolling waves. Magic or mirage?

Twenty-five kilometres from the coast is the small remote village of Aquaro, my paternal grandfather's village. Another five kilometres west of Aquaro, down a winding asphalt road, is my grandmother's village, Cosoleto. It is a region known for its olives, figs, chestnuts, brigands, saints, cautious and suspicious farmers (aren't all farmers suspicious?), unschooled shepherds, fresh air, spotless skies and refreshing, mountain-fed spring water.

Isolated and poor, the region preserved a way of life, attitudes, and culture not too distant from the Middle Ages, until the end of the Second World War. Until the early 1950s, donkeys were used for travelling up and down trails on market days. Feast days marked the rhythms of the agricultural year. Baskets made of bamboo leaves were used to collect olives.

It was in this rural landscape, not far from the coast, that the Filo family bought a parcel of land from Prince Ruffo.

The late eighteen and early nineteen hundreds were a period of confusion and insecurity for the Prince. Yes, he owned a large villa off the main piazza in Cosoleto, but he had spent most of his life loitering in the salons of Naples, enjoying fine clothes, food, music, and poetry. Poetry and wine were his tools of seduction.

The new librated times, however, made Prince Ruffo feel anxious and uncertain. The local population wanted land reform, and in a plebiscite had voted to join the North. French and Spanish troops were long gone and no longer available to round up troublemakers or to enforce arbitrary tax laws. Instead, there was a new country—Italy—and a national government led by Giovanni Giolitti, a crafty and unsavoury liberal who was using land reform to curry favour among the southern Italian peasants. Rather than give the land away, or have it taken from him, Prince Ruffo decided to sell it and remain for the rest of his days in Naples, the villa in Cosoleto be damned.

That very year, the gardens had been generous to the Filo family. A good potato yield and an unexpected bumper crop of winter wheat created enough extra liras to buy a small plot from Prince Ruffo. For his part, the Prince was only too happy to sell.

It was a bold step by the Filo family. The plot they were barely able to afford was remotely situated and thus hard to cultivate. It sat on an uneven slope of a mountain plateau, below the road leading to Gioia Tauro on the coast. Its remoteness had kept a patch of wild grapes hidden for over a hundred years.

It was here, many years later, that Sebastiano Filo found uncultivated grapevines growing along the edges of an old riverbed, the dull, purple fruit hidden under wide, green leaves. Curiosity and experimentation, the two dark horses of science (although Sebastiano never thought of himself as a scientist) led to luck. But what is luck, if not the unexplainable hand of fate?

Vitis vinifera, or the original grape, was from the Caucasus—at least, that is what the archaeological evidence indicates—and then it more or less spread across the Mediterranean after mingling with some variety of grapes in Croatia. A clone of Vitis, *Primitivo*, was thought to have been introduced into Southern Italy via the Puglia region in the eighteenth century. Don Francesco Fillippo Indellicati was the parish priest of the church at Gioia del Colle Bari. He selected an early plant of the Zagarese variety and grafted it to the Liponti. Cuttings from this clone were part of the dowry of the Contessa Sabini of Altamura when she married Don Tommaso Schiavoni of Maduria, the uncle of Prince Ruffo and the original landowner of what came to be Sebastiano's vineyard.

Did Sebastiano rediscover Primitivo? Did he graft a hybrid clone of Primitivo to the wild grape found at the bottom of a wide ravine?

The questions are part of the story. The lack of answers is part of the story. Weddings and wine are always part of a happy story. The names Sabini and Tommaso roll off the tongue and across the centuries like the clinking of wine glasses after the toast to the bride.

August 1967

The neighbourhood was changing, and so was I. A new avenue cut through the end of our street: six houses had been demolished to make way for the thoroughfare. I dreamed about Lucia—or sometimes about my grade six teacher Miss Brand. It resulted in a mess under my pyjamas, in both cases.

Lucia and her father, along with her Aunt Maria and Uncle Vince, had rented a cottage at Winnipeg Beach for a little summer holiday. My parents had also decided to rent there, and by coincidence, we were in the same block of wooden cottages that faced the highway on the edge of town, a stone's throw from the beach. Our families came together the way Italians in a new country often came together. They were each happy to find others who shared the same language and attachments to family, food, village life, and who understood the trials and tribulations of a new life in a new land. My mother, however, wanted to be left alone.

It was my father—careless, in my mother's eyes—who suggested our two families dine together every night. This made my mother furious. The last thing she wanted was to have to cook all the time, and for another family.

Exhausted from her piece work, cooking, shopping, cleaning, and a miscarriage, my mother was hoping for relief in the healing powers of sunshine and *aria fresca*, fresh air. She planned to rest at Winnipeg Beach, not to take part in a series of endless summer dinners. My father reasoned the opposite: she would have one less pot to stir. After all, Lucia's aunt also cooked. Besides, nothing pleased my father more than a boisterous meal. It was his defense against my mother's depression that like a vine on a pergola grew each year a little longer, a little darker, shading everything.

Lucia and I fell into each other's company and no one took notice. We chased each other on the sandy beach and into the lake. After supper we begged for money for a treat and then ran off to buy soft ice cream on cones at the boardwalk in town. We walked up and down ditches with an old minnow net, searching for frogs. Lucia gave each frog we caught a name before we let it go. Names like Paul, Sally, Ringo, or Julie.

I asked her how she knew which was a boy or a girl and she giggled.

—I just know.

I felt my face heat up at her answer, and saw the same little grin on her face that I'd noticed during our wanderings downtown with Hughie.

We decided one afternoon near the end of our vacation to follow the rail line to the grain elevator on the edge of town. Heat simmered off the railway tracks in waves, and the crushed rocks between the ties burned our heels. Bleached telephone poles stood against the empty bright blue sky except for a pair of crows drifting above us barely moving their wings.

We finally reached the grain elevator and sat down to rest in the shade. Two girls were walking towards us. We were both bored and hot so we thought we'd wait to see who they were. The air was still, the quiet broken only by the steady drone of crickets and the occasional angry buzz of a fly.

It was the older of the two girls who led us into the grain elevator. She said she wanted to show us something.

A wooden box materialized as if planned, and we scrambled up the raised iron ladder and slid through an opening on our stomachs. We tumbled, headfirst, into the grain. It was hot and dusty inside the elevator. Grain motes floated silently in the sunlight. The older girl, tall and thin, with blonde hair and freckled arms, walked over to a shady corner.

—Over here, she whispered.

We walked towards her as if pushing our way through snow, and stopped in front of her. She asked us to be quiet and to watch and then slowly, very slowly, she lifted up the front of her dress, scrunched it into a ball, and held it under her chin. We were now looking at her white underwear. Her head was tilted forward on a funny angle to keep the dress in place. She said nothing and stood silently, watching us watch her. Lucia and I knew instinctively what was expected, and a few moments later, followed her example. Next, the girl awkwardly pulled her underwear down, struggling to keep her dress tucked under her chin. Again, we followed her example. The three of us were now standing half-naked in front of each other, with our underwear and shorts around our ankles and our runners full of grain.

—Pull your shirt back so I can see, she said.

Embarrassed, I did as I was told. My penis and balls hung in the dry air. They felt separate from me, as if orphaned.

Satisfied with the view, the girl pointed first at me and then at her middle.

—A boy has a pointy thingy called a cocky. A girl has a

cunty. See?

I nodded. Out of the corner of my eye, I was trying to catch a glimpse of Lucia's middle, and to see what her reactions were to this bold statement. I was taken aback by this girl saying words normally said by older boys, and puzzled at her putting a *y* at the end of them. It was weird. Lucia seemed nonchalant. She had a studied look on her face, as if she were a scientist or a medical student, listening and watching with clinical attention. Unlike the freckled girl standing before me, Lucia's middle was covered in a fine, thin layer of pubic hair. I felt myself blushing, though no one seemed to notice.

The girl's friend casually glanced at all three of us, but didn't join in. I have to pee, she announced. She went over to a dark corner, stirring up more grain dust, and squatted.

I remained silent beside Lucia in the half-light, and looked at the girl standing in front of us. The two sides of her centre curved inward, parting like the opening of a small plastic change purse. I was unsure of what to say or do next. Her words and matter-of-fact tone had shocked me. The muffled hiss of pee hitting dry grain added to the feeling of taboo and mystery.

The lesson continued.

—A boy puts his inside a girl. Like this.

The tip of her baby finger disappeared. She was staring at me as she spoke, as if I was responsible for this villainy. I saw her lips tremble.

—In here is where babies are made. Did you know that?

It seemed she had a need to lord over us what she thought was our ignorance, or at the very least, wanted us to acknowledge her superiority, and to terrify us. It also seemed that she was out to prove she was mature and so-phisticated. We turned our heads from side to side.

—Well, now you know. I dare you to ask me a question.

Lucia and I said nothing. The other girl came over and giggled into her friend's ear.

It was becoming hot and stuffy and I badly wanted a glass of cold water. I could feel sweat forming on my brow and under my armpits.

Lucia suddenly spoke up.

—I have…ummm…well, it's not a question.

—What?

—I want to touch yours.

The girl nodded.

Lucia lightly grazed the girl's centre with her palm, as if she was touching a wounded bird. The other girl and I watched. It looked natural and no one dared make a sound. Then the older girl reached out and placed her hand on Lucia's centre, sighing and giggling at the same time. No one spoke.

The lesson was over in less than five minutes.

It felt like we had been standing there for an hour.

The older girl pulled up her underwear, lifted her chin, and let her summer dress roll down. We fell out of the elevator and took off down the road in opposite directions. Lucia and I ran in quick, abrupt bursts, almost falling. Lucia seemed wild. Her hair bounced off her shoulders. She opened her mouth and shouted. As we got closer to the cottages, we slowed to catch our breath, and fell silent. How could we talk about what had just happened? My own feelings were a mixture of shame, curiosity, excitement, and alarm. Lucia was as cool as an ice cube. Her blue-grey eyes dropped to avoid my questioning gaze.

—It was fun, Michael. I'm glad we met them.

—But, you…

—Oh grow up. Don't you dare say anything.

We walked the last thirty metres in silence. I felt foolish and thought Lucia must think I was a child.

Lucia's father and my parents were waiting for us, boiling over with anxiety and rage. They hollered at us. Where had we disappeared to for a whole afternoon?

—We were worried sick! said my mother. There are so many strangers here!

Then someone noticed bits of grain in my hair.

—I'll tan his skin black if he touched you, Lucia, yelled my father.

Lucia answered coolly and sweetly.

—Michael jumped off a haystack. She smiled.

—Sure he did, shouted her father. He delivered a series of quick, hard slaps to her face, knocking her head back.

—You dirty slut! I know what you've been doing. Get in the cottage!

It was our last night at Winnipeg Beach. My mother and Lucia's aunt had cooked all day to make a sumptuous meal to mark the end of our holidays together. After dinner, which Lucia missed, I sat on the back stoop of our cottage, wondering if she was okay, and trying to make some sense out of what had happened that afternoon. My mother, along with Lucia's aunt and uncle, had gone for a stroll on the boardwalk by the beach. Lucia's father and mine were chatting over a glass of wine. Thinking I was out of earshot, Domenico began to tell my father a story.

December 1940

The distant mountains appeared to be dipped in gold after the sunlight broke through the grey clouds. The light burned orange and red and magenta. He saw his friend Marino in front of him, slumped against a boulder, his intestines glistening. If Domenico had moved right instead of left a few seconds sooner, he would be like Marino, lying on the road cut open like a pig. Instead, he lay under some thick low bushes, legs bleeding, body flashing hot and cold.

He awoke in a tent, a dull throbbing in his head, his legs immobile, mouth dry. A weary doctor in need of a shave looked down on him; he spoke the sweet lyrical Italian of an educated Northerner.

—You are one of the lucky ones. We have enough morphine to get you out of here and on a ship back to Italy. It is the morphine that makes you thirsty. The war is over for you. That should please you. It will take some time but your wounds will heal. Nothing a few plates of pasta, sunshine, and wine cannot cure. But you should get your head checked in Italy.

It was December 10th, two days after the Feast of the Immaculate Conception.

The Virgin Mary had saved him.

He was half awake, and images and thoughts came and vanished. Clouds parted, and out poured merciful light. The Virgin Mary was on a white cloud. Behind her were shafts of light; at her feet, adoring children. The Virgin Mary spoke to him. She pointed to his mother and his sister hanging laundry on the small balcony facing the church of Santo Rocco di Aquarro. *Pray to me,* she said, *for forgiveness. The girl you beat in the olive groves after you fucked her, loves you.*

He saw the tears on his father's face when he learned his son was dead. But he was not dead. *I saved you,* said the Virgin Mary. He was aware that he was alive and in a tent, morphine numbing the pain in his legs and head. He asked for water and fell asleep.

Years later, he crossed the Atlantic to come to Canada. It was the third—and longest—boat ride of this life. The other two had been mere ferry rides across the Adriatic. On the first ferry ride he was standing: a knapsack, bedding and rifle on his back; both hands on the ship's rail looking out at the calm, flat sea. On the second, he was on his back, head bandaged, legs numb, strapped on a stretcher below the deck of a rusting fishing boat barely able to make port.

~~~

Lucia once showed me a photograph of her father, taken on his Atlantic crossing. He stood smiling and shirtless, one foot resting on a raised section of the deck; both hands relaxed atop his bent knee. His body was trim, almost thin.

—What you cannot see, Michael is the skin on his legs, riddled with small bumps of unevenly healed scar tissue. What you cannot see are the small bits of shrapnel in his head that were never removed.

Lucia continued.

—The raised scar tissue now and again throbs, and it always reminds him of the day the Virgin Mary saved his life on the morning of the Feast of the Immaculate Conception, on a deserted mountain road in the Pindus Mountains of Greece.

—What my father did not tell your father was that my mother was not on board. She was back in her mother's small kitchen, pregnant with me and waiting for her departure papers. She was sad, anxious, and excited to be moving to Canada with such a handsome husband—at least that is what my aunt told me. Her future was a blank page then: no one knows that she will die alone giving birth to me in a Winnipeg hospital on a cold, stormy, January night, leaving her already mentally wounded husband half-mad with grief and anger at his repeated bad luck, regardless of the Virgin Mary's intervention.

November 1971

The world was a big place and I wanted to be free and live my life the way I saw fit. I had no idea how the past could live in the present, and that one's desire to escape from family to anywhere and experience everything solved nothing.

At home I felt trapped but I felt guilty about thinking this way. My mother needed me.

My mother was unhappy, but I had no idea the cause nor the cure, nor did I really understand that she was clinically depressed. She could not get used to living in Canada, is what she told herself and anyone who cared to listen. My father rarely did, except to find fault with what he saw as her constant medical needs. He complained about her to his acquaintances and their unsympathetic wives, who meddled and offered useless advice.

—Ah, Carmela, we all have a cross to bear. Work. Keep busy. Look after your son. My husband is not much better, they told her. They would then mock her behind her back for not being strong, for being spoiled by her husband.

My mother had no words to explain her sadness. She always felt tired, and suffered from unexplainable aches and pains. Italy was the lost enchanted kingdom, the Eden from which she had been expelled by blind necessity and duty to her husband.

My father fled from my mother into an overtime of wrestling matches and card games. He never learned how to crack the black code of my mother's depression and was never able to control his rage at her constant medical needs.

I too wanted to break away: from the claustrophobic world of Italian family life, the constant worry and arguments, my mother's longing to return to a sunny Italy, away from the dark, cold winters.

The daily arguments between my parents at the dinner table resembled a mad physics where unseen and highly charged particles bumped against currents of confusion— about my mother's pills, her doctors, life in a new land, unpaid bills, work, school, fava beans, the price of meat, unforgiving winters, and the repeated axiom that absolutely no one was to be trusted.

I escaped to my books and the few record albums I could afford.

Hughie had gone, or so I thought. His family had moved out the summer Lucia and I were at Winnipeg Beach. Over the next few years I would hear scraps of information about him. He had dropped out of school. His brother Brian was in jail for punching out a cop. Hughie's family was living in a house in the North End, off Jarvis Street. He had been thrown out of Aberdeen School for stealing money from a teacher's purse. He was shoplifting jeans and records.

One evening he phoned.

—Hey Mikey, how've you been keeping? You still going to school?

—What the hell. Yeah, I'm still in school.

I noticed for the first time his rough edge, even though I'd always known it to be there. His matter-of-fact anger reminded me of his violent brother. I was also thinking about the rumours I'd heard about him running with a tough older crowd, spending a lot of time in pool halls.

He started explaining an idea he'd had. He wanted to sell my father's homemade wine to rubbies on Main Street. Although he sounded casual and cool over the phone, I sensed he was desperate. I wondered why he needed money so badly. We agreed on a time to meet.

It was a cold, windy, Saturday afternoon. He was waiting near the old Victorian fountain in Central Park, an Export A hanging from his lips, hands stuffed into the pockets of a bulky green army coat, collar up, bootlaces untied, cheeks and ears flushed red like a slab of uncooked beef.

—Jesus, what took you so long? I've been freezing my ass off, waiting. Got the wine?

—I had to wait till the coast was clear. The wine is kept in the basement and my mother was doing laundry there. You should wear a hat.

I handed him a briefcase with six bottles of wine

—Fuck off: a briefcase. Nice touch.

—I told them I was going to the downtown library to study. I'll walk with you to the end of the park. The wine is inside, in a shopping bag. I need the briefcase back.

Hughie now lived in an old red-brick apartment block

on Carlton Street near the edge of Central park. He spent his days hanging out at the pool hall at the corner of Arlington and Sargent. I knew the place. It had half a dozen pool tables, smoke-stained Venetian blinds that were never opened, terrible coffee, greasy chips, and a jukebox with an eclectic collection of 45s from the fifties and early sixties. Guys played pool for five bucks a game.

He told me school hadn't worked out for him. When we were kids, school for Hughie was either trouble or boring. As soon as he was old enough, he dropped out and made ends meet by working temporary at warehouse jobs. But his real passion was making fast money by selling hot goods. He'd started out stealing jeans at the Bay on Saturday afternoons—one tight pair fit under a baggy pair of Lee jeans— and then moved on to Rolling Stones and Led Zeppelin LPs, coats of all kinds, and small electronics like transistor radios. The bootlegging of wine was something new.

—I'll get you the money next week. Meet you at the statue in Eaton's.

After our meeting in the park, he started phoning every Sunday night to talk about life. I was too embarrassed to tell him about my interest in books, writing, and history. We talked instead about his drinking, shoplifting, dropping acid at parties, hanging out at the pool hall, girls. His cool factor was high and Hughie never lacked for girlfriends, or money for booze or drugs. But he wasn't trying to convince me of anything. It was more like he was testing our newfound friendship by telling me stories of his latest adventures in crime, or about some acid trip. There was a mocking tone to his voice, a challenge to the path I was on that was so opposite to his own. He wanted to know if I was still loyal to our shared childhood or whether I'd stuck to the straight and narrow. He was tempting me, offering me an alternative. He knew instinctively that I wanted to be somebody else. It was true. I wanted to be past my childhood, out of the old neighbourhood, away from my parents. I wanted to be away from the half-understood, half-articulated sadness and anger that hung over our house every day. Both fed my desire to run and be free of it all. How did he know?

~~~

Around the same time Hughie walked back into my life, I ran into Lucia again. It was the fourth of October, and I was on my way home from school, waiting for the 4:20 bus at the corner of Portage and Donald, to be exact. I had not seen her since our elementary school days.

She was wearing a black blazer with a large *A* and smaller *ST* on its breast pocket, gold spiked rays of holy light bursting from behind a small cross. St. Anne's. Her hair was tied back in a fat bundle and her blue-grey eyes, as always, were bright. She smiled a nervous hello.

—Lucia. Amazing. It's been awhile.

I was wearing my tie, half undone, and school football jacket. —Did you move? It's as if you disappeared.

She nodded. —At least six years ago. We moved to Sherburn Street at the end of elementary.

—Are you still living with your dad, and aunt and uncle?

—Yes, still with my father and crazy aunt. My uncle's okay, but I hate it; they watch me like a hawk.

—At least they let you take the bus to school and back, alone.

—They have no choice. We don't have a car and every-one works. It's so depressing. I'll be eighteen next year and my aunt still treats me like a child. My dad is worse. They both make me crazy.

I remembered the day her father slapped her after our show-and-tell adventure at the grain elevator.

Her father was known in the community as a man with a wild, bad temper and a paranoid imagination. He was *nervoso*, high strung, as were many Calabrian men, according to my mother. Domenico was especially feared whenever his anger flared. He was capable of anything, and had lost more than one job because of it, once throwing a shovel at the foreman's head at a construction site. And one time he had picked up a meat cleaver in a social-hall kitchen, and chased a young man down the street after he'd seen him smiling and talking to Lucia.

Lucia and I sat together at the back of the bus. The bus turned onto Balmoral, a street lined with shabby houses, then headed north for three blocks before turning onto Sargent. It travelled west, past Woolworth's and Safeway, the legion, a second-hand bookstore where I often bought cheap paperbacks, a hardware store, and the empty outdoor con-crete pool the two of us used to play in. I missed my stop to travel with her as far as Arlington in front of the Towne Cin-ema, but I didn't dare get off with her, afraid her father might see me.

Over the next few weeks, the warm fall weather turned cool and she began wearing navy-blue V-necked sweaters that emphasized the curve of her breasts under her school jacket. The late afternoon light looked paler, and long shadows fell across the sidewalks. Orange and yellow leaves littered the streets and cold, windy days became more frequent. The lurching stop-and-start of the bus pushed and brushed us together, and while we talked, the city at the end of the day gradually turned into a black-and-white photograph.

And a reasonable question to ask at this point is why? What force drew Lucia's hand towards mine, to guide it under her skirt, past her thigh towards her panties and onto her soft pubic hair, the movement concealed by the pink school binder on her lap and my black leather briefcase propped on both our knees. A pressed smile formed on her face as she searched my face for an answer.

You could say I liked her ever since elementary school days, but back then it was the way a boy likes a candy bar and without much thought. You could also say we had shared a secret from our summer at Winnipeg Beach. You could say that desire was sitting under our skin, and that uncertainty (mine) and confusion (mine again) and curiosity (mine and hers) had mixed with her bold, youthful quest for knowledge.

It was plain to everyone that Lucia was pretty. Pretty, young Italian girls required vigilance. Lucia was motherless and this created its own special cross, according to her aunt. And just as I was trying to escape from my mother's depression and the illness that blanketed our house like a layer of impenetrable volcanic ash, Lucia was trying to escape from the tyranny of her jealous and paranoid father. She was never to challenge or, worse, talk back to her father. She was expected to blindly respect the demands, customs, and traditions of her Southern Italian family. Except that her father's repression acted like an elixir on Lucia.

She saw me as a fellow escape artist, a guy who wanted

to be part of a larger world with his love of books and history. I saw her as soulful and sad, a girl who longed to be free, excited to share her beautiful body. And I wanted to be more than just a respectable high school kid, cocooned and trapped inside the dull routines of school. Intuitively we believed we could break the chains that held us in place. We didn't know it then, but we were both caught in the eternal triangle of youthful rebellion, desire, and curiosity.

It goes without saying that I fell in love with her after she guided my hand over her warm thighs.

Early 1900s

I am descended from the Maldenti and Filo clan: the grandson of Rosalina Maldenti and of Sebastiano Filo, an ordinary man who grafted the local *Greco Nero* onto a pale, purple grape no one had ever seen before, and became famous.

As a young man Sebastiano had flirted with the local Calabrian brigands, but his spirit and character didn't lend itself to the violence expected of him. He was not a mean, calculating man; rather, he was pragmatic about the business of working and living. His spirit was closer to that of an ignored poet, and he preferred the quiet art of tending vineyards and gardens than the robust, sly, and larger-than-life existence of an outlaw.

He never drew attention to himself or caused a stir (although this was to change). Still, he was pleased when he received a letter from a wealthy landowner congratulating him on his able work in the owner's vineyards. Sebastiano was well known for his ability to transform a vineyard, to make a grape that was *dolce e allegro*, sweet and playful, and for his ability to create new types of wine by grafting. You could say he was an artist, a wine sculptor, who in his tending and shaping and layering of a vineyard, produced not a sculpted bronze, but something equally beautiful and satisfying: a fine barrel of wine.

Sebastiano married young. He was nineteen, and Rosalina, one of three village beauties, was only sixteen. She stood no more than five feet, with thick, wavy, auburn hair and intense black eyes. Full bosomed at fifteen, she walked to the fields, head held high, proud of her thin Minoan waist and ample breasts. She was Sebastiano's opposite. It was said her eyes flashed hot like coals when she was angry and shone like sunlight when she laughed. Piety and modesty, virtues valued in saints and the Madonna, found no place in her spirit. It was whispered her flashes of stubborn anger were inherited from her father, Carmine Maldenti, the feared brigand.

The vineyards in Calabria were organized and planted wherever there was sufficient land and an angled southern exposure for the grapes to absorb the strong Mediterranean sun. The land Sebastiano Filo inherited from his family was not a large *vigna*, but more of a *vignetto*, a small vineyard, in a forgotten and abandoned corner of the Prince's estate. After careful study he decided the slope was gentle enough to begin the arduous task of removing the wild bushes and scrub-growth and tilling the soil before the planting could begin and later the grafting.

Sebastiano was nineteen or twenty when he grafted the small, useless-looking, pale-plum-coloured grape he discovered there onto a fat purple one the locals called *Greco Nero*, the Black Greek, for the jet-black colour it turned when pressed. The Greco Nero grape was not that different from the Malvasia grape that had been in the Mediterranean basin for centuries, and produced a strong wine called *Il Ciro*. The hybrid grape that resulted had light-mauve skin and was ruby fleshed within, the reverse of most grapes. The dark interior gleamed with small triangular shards of light. After two or three glasses of the wine it produced, imbibers erupted into careless dance, disheveled dress (clothes suddenly feeling uncomfortable and constricting), and impulsive behaviour.

Eventually those extraordinary grapes and the wine they produced would land Sebastiano on the streets of New York with his evening's spending money tucked under his tongue. Later still, he would find himself in a whorehouse in the city of Buffalo—and not long after, was waving to his brother from a third-class train compartment reeking of over-ripe cheese and sour whiskey heading for Winnipeg, and wondering what he had done and who was in hot pursuit.

The new wine had changed everything, but no one knew how, especially Sebastiano. All he could recall while sitting in the train's cold compartment as it headed north was playing Scopa on a quiet afternoon at the Café Savoy, not far from a tumble of other broken and weary hotels, on a quiet afternoon in Buffalo.

February 1919

The neighbourhood whores were asleep in their rooms after a boozy Saturday night. The afternoon light was flat and dull.

A thin cloud of blue cigarette smoke hung above the card tables. The men played for a glass of wine at the end of each hand and dreamed of the Sunday afternoon pasta dinners they used to eat back home with their families. The Filo brothers had lost five hands in a row. Antonio suggested their tablemates change seats to break their losing streak, and offered to pay up with some of his own wine, hidden in a hip flask. He was hoping to avoid paying the café's price for wine (he needed to save his money to send to his mother back home), and he was hoping the magic of Sebastiano's wine would turn his luck around. But after the third offering from his flask, it all turned out wrong. A fist on the table… shouts from the other men…the café owner slapping his thighs, in horror and anger…blood spattering…in someone's chest, a knife.

To this day no one is sure exactly what happened. Who started the fight? What set them off? The cards? The wine? And how did Sebastiano come to be on the train?

But the answer, of course, was the wine. The wine connected to the hybrid grape, which was connected to the gypsies, who were connected to the villages of Southern Calabria scattered like salt across the plateaus of the blue Apennine Mountains, these villages connected to the Saracen attacks, that were connected to the original Ancient Greek settlements, and so on and so on, until one cold January day in 1919, three months before the Winnipeg General Strike and four years after he and Antonio had set foot on Ellis Island outside New York Harbor, Sebastiano arrived alone at the CPR Station in Winnipeg.

The only thing certain was that the wine, grafted from the orphan grape, had changed everything.

Back in Italy, Rosalina's infamous temper exploded when she heard that her husband was trapped in the middle of a frozen continent. Her rage swept through the house like a tempest when she learned the only way they were going to be reunited and could start a family together was if she braved crossing the Atlantic.

She never did leave and instead, like Penelope, waited and waited until he returned, ignoring the glances and smiles of the men in the village.

The rest, as they say, is history. History is a bellhop arriving with half the luggage, or as is often the case, an indistinct figure grinning in the half-light of a street lamp. The wine had sent Sebastiano away (again) to live and work in windswept Winnipeg.

1972

Lucia and I started meeting at the Cornish Library on West Gate. We stayed away from our old haunts downtown, like the Paddlewheel Restaurant at the Bay, for fear of running into anyone who might know us.

The bus to the library went straight down Maryland Street, past a mix of old three-storey homes with big verandas, converted now into rooming houses; square apartments in hues of red, white, or brown, and stained with grime; and houses that looked like sad, squalid wallflowers. Maryland Street, old and bruised, had at one a time been a desired location for Winnipeg's middle and upper class. Many of the houses now had dingy curtains or a Confederate flag in their windows.

My stop was at Westminster United Church, its neo-Gothic spires spiking upward like the pictures I'd seen of the tower at Magdalene College in Oxford (and no doubt alluding to it). One of the 1919 General Strike leaders, James Wordsworth, had lived a block further on, near the corner of the Maryland Bridge. It was there that the army had set up a sandbag nest for a machine gun, fearing strikers might at any moment mimic their crazed Russian Bolshevik brethren and make a bloodthirsty rush across the bridge to ransack the stately homes of Wellington Crescent and murder their occupants. I knew that my grandfather had been in Winnipeg during that time, and although he hadn't participated in the strike or the demonstrations, I felt a kinship or historical connection to those events. It was only when I was older that I learned about the wine.

I usually arrived before Lucia. I savoured the silence and calm inside: the library like a secular cathedral, with its gleaming hardwood floors and the smell of Pine-Sol and floor wax. I'd wait for her at a massive oak table behind the shelves of atlases in the corner by the washrooms. Almost no one ventured into this area, except for the occasional grade six student bent on learning the names of all the capital cities east of the Danube River. The two of us held hands and studied, pausing now and then to give each other deep, long kisses. Sometimes I kissed her because I was bored of reading my notes. Sometimes I kissed her just for the thrill of feeling her lips and the desire that ran between us like a current and lit up every nerve cell. Lucia would squirm and eventually push me back gently, eyes shining with delight, both of us disoriented for a moment after we disconnected, as though emerging from an underwater swim.

One day, we discovered an old path behind the library that ran along the edge of the riverbank. The path was no wider than a cat and cut through tall wild grass, scrub bushes, and the thick trunks of old oaks and elms. Sunlight flashed through the leaves above us. The Assiniboine River flowed by, slow and grey-green.

The path opened out onto a small clearing. Tucked away in an overgrown corner and hidden from view by a small bend in the river was a dock made of wide, weathered planks. Beside it was a brick patio overrun with moss and weeds that grew between the cracks. It appeared that neither had seen use for years. We spread a picnic blanket on the moss-encrusted patio to eat lunch.

Under the elms, Lucia burst like a ripe apricot.

1938

My father Nino did not ask himself if it was necessary to marry. He wanted to marry. The idea of marriage came to him simply and naturally, like the distracted and casual way his brother Giovanni had tossed the end of a scarf over his shoulder, the night before he left for Rome. It was like asking why the sun is hot in July. Quite simply, the sun is hot, and neither he nor the sun had any choice in the matter, in the same way a man has no choice but to work for a living.

The year was 1938 and it would be two years before my father went to war. Fourteen years after the war ended, he would be on the bleak and windswept corner of Logan and Isabelle in Winnipeg, desperate to rent rooms before his wife and son arrived. But on this bright July day, Nino merely understood that marriage and work were inescapable facts of life.

He had seen his bride-to-be—although she herself did not know his intent—for the first time six months earlier, as she and her sister washed laundry on the outskirts of the village with the other women. He noted her round cheeks and dark brown eyes and the way her unadorned hair fell and curled against her neck. The other women, in contrast, wore their hair in tight braids pinned and tucked under sweat-stained bands of light-coloured cloth.

Nino continued to watch her day after day. His flock would announce his presence before his arrival, the sheep mournfully bleating ahead of him. This gave the women time to collect their wits and ignore him. Nino, for his part, would look down from the road above and tip his hat in their direction, whether they looked up or not. Sometimes they nodded their heads curtly and quickly returned to their laundry. Nino, not to be outdone, would turn away and pause to look out at another cloudless blue sky and at the morning mist rising up off the distant mountains.

He had come to learn that Carmela was not a woman of the olive groves, orchards, or gardens like most of the other women in the village. Other than on laundry days, she seldom ventured far from her home. She cooked, cleaned, washed and mended clothes. She fed the chickens in front of the house, taking delight in how they ran towards her when she arrived every morning with crumbs and scraps from yesterday evening's meal. She rarely smiled, but when she did, it was a shy crease of resignation.

On this day, the woman spread out along the stream, each working in front of her own smooth rock. The sharp slaps of cloth against the wet stones sounded like a savage beating.

—What is he stopping to look at? He looks lost, yet he's crossed that path since he was a boy. What is he doing now? Staring at the mountains?

—He's staring at nothing; he's waiting for us to say something. He thinks we should admire his looks. Ignore him.

The women returned to their laundry and Nino returned to his flock, half dreaming and half thinking about what to do next. He was in no position to make his intentions known. He was part of a long line of peasants who had worked the land for centuries. At sixteen his heart was an unfinished poem. He shrugged his shoulders at the women below and started down the road out of Cosoleto.

At that very moment, unknown to Nino, rumours were spreading across the mountain villages and down into the terraced olive treed valleys that an ancient and potent wine had been rediscovered and inexplicably filled men's hearts with love or rage.

1783

The present-day location of the village of Cosoleto sits 440 feet above sea level on a small plateau that slants towards the plain of Gioia, which eventually meets the sea. The plateau is like a wide finger vertically planted on the slope of one of the low Apennines Mountains. Cosoleto is about sixty kilometres from Reggio di Calabria, the regional capital, which is reputed to possess (according to the early twentieth century poet d'Annunzio) the most beautiful boardwalk along the sea in all of Italy.

You find Cosoleto, however, by leaving the splendour

of Reggio and driving north along the coastal Autostrada del Sole to the small fishing village of Bagnara. Once there, you turn inland, away from the sea, and drive on a narrow secondary road that twists and turns and rises and falls, and appears designed to force you to find out if you've made peace with your lunch, or your maker.

The broken remains of the former Cosoleto sit at the bottom of a deep gorge. There is no boardwalk or stunning view of the sea here. Depending on where you are in the village, the view is either of ravines filled with wild chestnut trees and low shrubs, or of dark mountain peaks that jut into a clear blue sky.

The gorge itself is the result of five destructive earthquakes, followed by tsunamis, that hit Calabria and Sicily in early 1783.

~~~

The first earthquake began with a weak rumbling around eight in the morning of February 5th. It was first felt along the coast but was barely noticed at inland villages such as Cosoleto. The first tremor was quick and brief, like a small orgasm; then nothing. The men and women in the fields around Cosoleto noted the movement, and although normally suspicious of any sudden change in the natural world (it was reported later that vast flocks of startled birds took flight), the field workers themselves took no notice. The tremor stopped as suddenly as it had started and everyone returned to their work. The sun was shining; the sky a crisp, spotless blue.

At Scylla, the fishing village on the west coast—the one

with the famous promontory extending into the water and old Norman castle perched on top—the sea unexpectedly withdrew from the shore, exposing the marine floor. Not long afterwards, the sea came rolling back in, boiling and frothing as if overheated. Hundreds of fish washed up on the rocky beach and lay dead in the curling surf. Here, too, the inhabitants were puzzled but not alarmed, although a few wary fishermen refused to put out to sea. In the meantime, the poorest of the villagers rushed out to collect the fresh dead fish.

Around noon, the first of several violent earthquakes hit (there were to be a total of five over the next four weeks), and what followed was the most destructive seismic crisis Calabria had seen in over two thousand years. The territory's geography—its mountains, valleys, hills, plateaus, creeks and river systems—were rearranged. Springs dried up and new ones appeared. Water was diverted from long-established riverbeds, and fresh waterways were created. Fissures and clefts of various depths and widths indiscriminately swallowed up churches, homes, animals, trees, and in some cases, whole villages. Roads came to an abrupt end or vanished altogether. Landslides damned up streams and produced lakes. Trees were uprooted and people tending their gardens were knocked down.

Cosoleto itself shook violently, like an enraged father who has just learned his eldest daughter has stained the family's honour. The elderly, the sick, mothers and children—in other words, all those not working the fields and olive groves—rushed outside their homes as walls cracked and roofs collapsed. They stood huddled together, uncertain what to do. Some beseeched the sky for mercy. A few women ran out to the fields, their long black skirts pulled up past their ankles. The bakery chimney collapsed, then caught fire. The ground cracked and fissures appeared, twisting and turning unevenly. When the earth grunted once more, the openings expanded into deep, long gashes.

Gypsies had set up camp outside the village the night before. They were travelling from town to town in the interior of Calabria in dirt-caked, patched, canvas-covered wagons, peddling clay and brass-bottomed cooking pots, iron candlesticks, bolts of colourful cloth and silk, hand-woven carpets, straw brooms, intricately carved axe handles, and small purple bottles (filled with love potions, they claimed). They also offered to tell the future. If money in a town was scarce, they bartered, accepting a handkerchief full of tomatoes, a small bag of dried beans, even a basket of grapes.

The gypsy women were preparing lunch when the earth shook and the crash of walls and the shouts and screams began. The gypsy men ran up the road and saw women, children, and old men scurrying about like ants on a destroyed anthill. Clouds of dust hovered in the air. Below ground, the earth's persistent growls and grumbles sounded like a menacing animal. On the steps of the village church, its roof collapsed, were a group of six or seven women and children: before them, a large open sinkhole where there used to be a road. Trapped, the children sobbed and the women wailed like cats on a moonless night.

A few gypsy men rushed over to help them, but the women rejected their efforts—they refused to be saved by an unchristian gang of thieves and layabouts. More fissures appeared. The village fountain split and water began to spread throughout the streets. A loud crack followed, as if someone had torn away the earth with one sharp pull. A row of homes weaved as if drunk, then collapsed.

In an uncharacteristic show of selflessness (or perhaps they saw some advantage to rescuing the town's women and children), the men ran back to their camp and returned, pulling one of their wagons. They ripped planks from its sides and threw them overtop the fissures.

First, a young mother clutching a baby ran across. Then another woman crossed, dragging two young children howling with fear. One by one, the trapped villagers crossed over from the church, weeping at the indignity of having to be saved by gypsies. At the same time, a mudslide erupted from the plateau and swept away the unattended wagon in a cocktail of mud, bricks, and uprooted olive trees. The cart eventually stopped at the bottom of what had once been the banks of a small stream, and was buried in a mound of fresh alluvial soil.

Over time, the rich silt that had been carried by the old stream down the mountainside, mixed well with the enriched soil brought to the surface by the earthquake. Coincidentally, a basket of grapes inside the wagon also mixed well with the loamy soil.

As for the earthquake, for centuries it remained in the minds of the local population as a manifestation of God's fury: punishment for the countless sins committed by the people of the South.

And as for the vines that sprang up, to be discovered later by Sebastiano, they were the prelude to decades of trouble for my family.

1972

On Friday nights before hitting the bars, Hughie liked to relax at the Diamond Pool Hall on Notre Dame. It was at the bottom of a flight of stairs in a building between Home Street and Simcoe. Here, there were three pool tables, a couple of pinball machines, and a small office with a desk, chair, and cashbox. The stripped remains of a black motorcycle in perpetual repair sat near the office. Beside it were two wheel caps, full of nuts, bolts, and a few sparkplugs. In another pile was a tangle of chrome and cables.

The kid who managed the place was a skinny guy in his late twenties. He usually sat with his feet up on a table, gazing motionless at a black-and-white portable TV. He ignored the customers except when they tilted the pinball machines or when he heard the crack and bang of a cue ball knocked off a table.

—Hey! Play pool not baseball!

I was a lousy pool player. My shots weren't crisp and clean, and I held the cue by pushing it through a hole I made by curling my forefinger over my thumb, or by attempting to rest it in the uneven *V* between my thumb and index finger. I could not, like Hughie, spread and arch my hand upward on the table to effortlessly guide the cue and make a precise well-calculated shot.

I had been hearing less and less from Hughie. He stopped calling on Sunday nights to ramble on about his life or to take sarcastic shots at mine. Hughie knew it was not a great idea to visit my house. My father disliked him and called him *un bumbo.*

Hughie was no longer a kid eating hotdogs whenever he

felt like it. His style of freedom no longer appealed to me and I now suspected it to be sleazy and hollow. I used to love wandering around downtown aimlessly with him and later to stop and drink malts together at the Met and secretly watch girls dip french fries into small paper cups filled with ketchup. It was a thrill that hinted at freedom, coupled with the slow burn of youthful desire. I had admired his confidence and the swagger of a young thief.

That was all gone, yet our friendship somehow lingered. He now had a reputation for being mean and tough. He was scary, the way his brother was scary. But I also had changed. I thought that Lucia and I could together strike out into the world: to be ourselves, free of the straitjacket of Southern Italian family life.

But one evening Hughie did call, and I met him at the Diamond.

—Mikey, I need a partner. Someone who won't rip me off. You and I are old pals; I know we can work together. It'll be easy cash while you're still in school. Think about it.

He took a drag from his cigarette and whispered the last sentence close to my ear while exhaling smoke from his nostrils. There was something about this gesture that brought back memories, and scenes from my childhood flashed through my mind as he talked. Hughie and I used to play 'Guns' on summer afternoons. We were eleven-year-olds with cowboy six-shooters from Eaton's. Sometimes we'd take turns using a fake World War II German Luger. We'd hide behind bushes or creep along the side of a house, imagining ourselves a cunning Vic Morrow from *Combat* or a dashing sharpshooter outwitting outlaws and the Apache, like Randolph Scott or John Wayne. *Horse Opera* on CBC was our favourite TV show and we watched it without fail every Saturday afternoon.

But the gesture annoyed me. This bit of movie melodrama may have worked with the small-time thugs he hung out with on the street, but to me it seemed phony. I wondered how many people he had conned. I'd heard he did 'crazy' extremely well on the street.

—Your dad's wine is amazing. Can you get more? We can double the price.

~~~

My father's wine cellar was a converted pantry in our basement. The shelves were lined with a jumble of old Mason jars, big brown jugs, and rum and whiskey bottles holding wine samples from each year. Hoses for sucking wine out of the barrel when it got low hung loosely from a nail, like dead snakes. There were two grey tin funnels, a scattered collection of corks and black liquor caps of varying shapes and sizes, and a wine-stained yellow bucket for catching any spillage.

Every September from the time I was about twelve, I had helped my father make wine. We'd go together to Di Santo's, the Italian grocery store at the corner of Furby and Sargent, to look through the cases of black Zinfandel grapes that had arrived from faraway California. My father would paw through the flimsy, white plywood crates stained purple with grape juice. Before buying, he always argued over the quality and amount of the grapes in each box.

— So what, it's stamped ten pounds; it feels like two kilos only. Why should I believe what it says on the box?

Ugo, the store's owner, found my father exasperating but was used to his theatrics, and accepted it as part of the cost of doing business with him.

—Nino, go to my scales and weigh a box yourself.

—Why should I believe your scales?

Once it was clear he had lost the weight argument, my father would then point at two or three damaged grapes (obviously bruised by workers trying to pack as many grapes as possible into the small box) or a few that were slightly spoiled after being hauled by truck halfway across North America.

—Look at this box. Half the grapes are rotten.

His next move would be to casually pluck a few grapes at random, as if he were a customs inspector, pop them into his mouth, then hastily spit them out with disgust.

—You call these grapes! They taste like dull lemons full of weak acid.

The purpose of all this grandstanding, both my father and Ugo knew, was to lower the price of the grapes.

—*Porco Dio*, pig-god, Nino! You want me to gift you the grapes? They are the best. Christ and all the angels in heaven could not give you a better price.

My father, however, never relented or admitted he was performing. He did not trust Ugo Di Santo; the man's perceived greed galled him. In his mind the price asked for the grapes was always too much, and whether they were quality grapes or not was irrelevant to his goal of getting a lower price. Plus, he was a Northerner from Friulani, and a Northerner must never be allowed to outsmart a Southerner like my father.

—Who knows what he really pays per shitty box? he would tell my exasperated mother who, after all the arguing and insults between the two men, would be sent to finally settle on a price. A few days later, twenty-five boxes of plump, purple Zinfandel grapes would arrive. My father and I would unload them from the half-ton delivery truck, one box at a time, and carry them to the basement to be washed. Soon the whole house would take on the rich, sweet scent of ripe grapes.

We would already have cleaned out the enormous, wooden wine barrels, using old wine and a bit of sulfur to kill any invisible fungus growing in the wood before hosing them down again to expand the wood and remove any remaining sulfur. My father would attach the grape crusher—a contraption that looked like a big meat grinder—to the lip of an open barrel. My job was to feed the grapes into the crusher while he turned the handle to operate the metal roller inside. The grapes would be mashed by the roller's medieval-looking spikes and plop down with a wet, sickening splash into the barrel. Sometimes we took turns, either cranking the roller, or picking up the boxes and pouring them over the grinder. I thought it was peasant work and resented it. My father was demanding. He shouted about how slow I was in bringing over each box of grapes. He shouted that we had to finish today or all the grapes would rot overnight. He shouted that I knew nothing about work, about how my mother had spoiled me. My muted anger simmered under my skin.

In a week or so, the crushed grapes would have begun to boil or ferment. After the fermenting stopped, we'd put the wine through a wine press, strain it, and then pour it into another barrel for storage. By early December, the wine would be ready to drink.

~~~

The days were passing one on top of the other like the cards I used to toss against our garage wall. I looked out at the trees and hedges stretched in front of the houses, and the line 'I may as well try and catch the wind' ran through my head. Three months and high school would be over. I didn't know what I was going to do. I wanted to go away, to escape to McGill University in Montreal, to travel with Lucia. I had not told my parents I would be leaving. And I needed money.

It had been weeks since I last saw Lucia. I knew something was wrong.

She called from a pay phone inside the Safeway store where she had a part-time job as a cashier. Her usual breezy attitude was replaced with a tone of quiet urgency. It was very important; she needed talk to me, was all she said.

I agreed to meet her at the Salisbury House restaurant at the corner of Arlington and Notre Dame later that day, after her shift.

Events were piling up fast, one on top of the other. I had to take the afternoon off from school to help my mother go by bus downtown to see Dr. Albo, her quack Italian doctor (and the only physician in the city who was fluent in Italian). My mother had complained that winter of headaches and burning sensations all over her body. Her legs and arms ached and she was sensitive to any change in the weather.

I knew her health had been an issue from the first day she arrived in Winnipeg. She had endured the boat ride across the Atlantic and the train ride across half the country, but to arrive in this windy city along the banks of the Red and Assiniboine Rivers when the snow still lay five feet deep, was too much for her. She couldn't believe her husband had wanted her to come to such an inhospitable place. She felt tricked and cheated, and her resentment had begun that day in late February 1959 when she stepped off the train, wearing a thin grey wool coat, a stylish red-and-blue scarf, and black pumps. Under her coat she wore a light sweater and a modest, pale blue spring frock. The cold was unlike anything she had ever experienced: it felt like a wound. The gold of the afternoon winter light and the starkness of the empty trees looked make-believe. She started to cry. She was exhausted from her long journey and from caring for me, and she was homesick. She was surprised to see white exhaust pouring from the rear of cars, and that the unblemished blue sky looked Mediterranean. My father hadn't thought to bring blankets to keep us warm and this added to her disappointment. Her sister Rosa waited stoically while he filled the trunk and then the car's back seat with all their luggage.

My mother retold this story on the bus, her tone dropping with resignation one minute and rising with bitter but soft-spoken regret the next: about leaving the warm sunshine and fresh air of Italy and the familiar comfort of her parents' home for the frozen winters of Canada and a feckless husband. She paused and smiled for a moment, and mentioned the day I had tossed a small white ball with blue stars to the Mediterranean dolphins that had followed the ship. My mother, like many rural Southern Italian women of her generation, clung to the notion that, regardless of whatever hardship you had to endure or whatever pleasure or wealth you desired or earned, your family came first, especially your children.

Her devotion to family angered me, yet at the same time it made me feel disloyal to her and guilty about my secret longing to escape. I saw my mother's view of life as narrow, duty bound, dull and cautious. I wanted to see and experience the world for myself. I wanted a full and interesting life. A virtuous life with a job, a mortgage, wife and children, was a boring life.

As usual, I kept my feelings to myself and watched for our stop. I never argued with my mother, and besides, we were on a bus in full view of everyone. I had learned to be a polite Canadian after all.

We got off at the Bay and walked the remaining block to the Boyd Building, trying to avoid the frozen puddles broken by footprints. The city, as always, was a ragged ruin in springtime. The scattered remains of winter were everywhere: soggy and faded cigarette packages, candy wrappers, Styrofoam cups, gritty sand, dog shit, a green wool sock on a sewer lid. Yellowed newspaper pages and transfer tickets lay under clumps of slush. The entire avenue appeared to be a vast archeological record of a careless race of people hard pressed by winter. My mother cursed the cold wind that came at us from three different directions, and shook her head with disgust at the mess on the street.

We sat down in the reception area to wait. In front of us was a coffee table topped in casual disorder with women's magazines, their cover headlines remote from my mother's life: 'The Three-Step Grilled Cheese Sandwich,' 'New Hair and a New You,' 'Lose Weight Faster and Keep It Off Longer.' She quietly flipped through some of them, murmuring approval or disapproval of the latest women's fashions. She had been a seamstress back in her village, and was known for her accurate eye and neat stitching. She could transform an old dress or shirt into something new and fresh.

A nurse escorted us to an examination room, barren except for a narrow bed lined with beige paper. When Dr. Albo finally arrived he asked me to wait outside. I spent the rest of the afternoon taking my mother from lab to lab for the bunch of tests he ordered. We returned home, exhausted, to await the results.

1914

Sebastiano's new wine did not assert itself right away, nor did anyone in particular notice its qualities. It was Sebastiano's younger brother, Antonio, who noted the power and confidence it gave some people, while others were overcome with unexplainable passions and desires. It was an unexpected powerful new wine (and find) made from the hybrid Greco Nero grape—cultivated on a mound created by an earthquake situated on land that Prince Ruffo, the local landowner, had deemed worthless because it sloped on a forty degree angle—by none other than his modest and retiring older brother. It was only natural that after discovering its unusual effect, Antonio would form a scheme to use the wine for his own purposes.

Unlike Sebastiano, Antonio was a man of appetites. He was robust, handsome and broad-shouldered, with black, wavy hair and dark brooding eyes. He preferred the solid work of a stonecutter or blacksmith to the gentle, steady work of market gardening or tending vineyards. He was also a natural entrepreneur. He thought nothing of travelling all day by mule to the nearby villages to sell whatever extra produce the family had grown. It was an easy way to meet and flirt with pretty girls who wandered about the market stalls to buy or to escape the watchful eye of their parents. Antonio's trips into the surrounding countryside and along the coast were responsible, on more than one occasion, for a father from a distant village arriving at the Filo family doorstep, anxious to discuss with the parents of *il grande signor Antonio* the young man's intentions regarding his daughter. It was always a moment fraught with tension and unbearable embarrassment, and usually concluded with shouts and threats by the angry father when he finally understood Antonio's mother's assertion that her son's proposal was worthless.

—Perhaps…and I say this respectfully, perhaps it was your daughter who misunderstood my son? Besides, he is still only a boy. He is hardly ready for marriage; he has no money. And we need him here under our roof.

And yet again, another prospective father-in-law was sent away crestfallen and seething. Once the man was far enough from the house, Antonio's mother would start to yell, threatening to pluck out Antonio's eyes with her cooking spoon, to cut out his silver tongue and to sever his cock, to chop them into a thousand pieces and feed them to the pigs.

—But she was so beautiful…

—Quiet, you bastard. You think all young women are beautiful. Stop or you will pay in blood.

Antonio, for his part, would drop his eyes and mumble a rash promise to never again propose marriage to an innocent village girl.

Easily bored, restless, Antonio looked for ways to pass the empty evenings in this small, obscure village perched on a plateau under the blue-peaked Apennines Mountains. On dull, warm evenings after supper, men gathered in the café across from the church to drink wine, or on lazy, hot afternoons after Sunday Mass when half the village was enjoying a *pisaolino*, a little nap, the other half loitered quietly in the shade. The younger men preferred to play *Scopa*, To Sweep, in groups of four, one pair of partners pitted against another pair. The rules were simple: the pair who lost a round was required to buy a glass of wine for each man on the winning team, a not particularly onerous hardship, wine being plentiful and cheap. But after a few hours of this, an idle, friendly card game could become operatic, the easy banter sharp and bitter, as partners and opponents alike accused each other of incompetence or stupidity.

One evening near the end of May 1914, Rocco Lupino stood across from Antonio and asked if he and his cousin Angelo could play a few hands before supper. It had been a hot day, the heat by mid-morning already oppressive. In the distance, a zappa struck the dry, red earth in a slow, steady, mechanical beat.

Rocco, as everyone knew, had just returned from Naples where he had spent the last six years in jail for attempted murder. He looked well turned out compared to the dusty young men seated outside the café. He wore light flannel pants and a dark jacket on his narrow shoulders. Underneath was a clean white shirt, neatly pressed and starched, but too large for his slender frame. His polished black shoes were new and his belt had a shiny silver buckle. On his right hand was a gold ring with an *R* in its centre. The pinky fingernail beside it was long and filed neatly into the shape of an exquisitely sharp nib. Someone had obviously spent a pretty penny on him, and Rocco was showing off, letting everyone know he was back in business—and it was not the business of hoeing gardens or herding sheep.

Rocco put a lit cigarette in the corner of his mouth and poured smoke through his nostrils like a dragon. He watched the card players in a studied but casual manner, as if he were watching a pretty woman pass by on the street.

Antonio looked up from his cards and glanced over at Rocco without breaking the rhythm of the game. Antonio disliked this type of man: a lazy man by nature, who played the role of being a superior and prosperous genteel landowner but who, in reality, used fear and intimation to make his money. The new clothes didn't hide the fact that Rocco looked like a corpse, despite the best efforts of his mother to bring him home-cooked meals in prison. Although he moved his hand nonchalantly to his mouth to remove his cigarette, he still gave the impression that his nerves were coiled. He looked, in essence, like a well-dressed madman.

—Of course, Rocco. Have a seat. You gentlemen know how we play. A glass of wine each round. No IOUs. You remember Pepe, Frank's son. Their bakery is behind the old Ruffo villa. You look well, Rocco.

—Thank you, Antonio. Always polite. How is the family?

—Good, thanks. And yours?

You can see their meeting was courteous and the tone was pleasant and followed custom.

So what force drew Rocco to seat himself across from Antonio that day and to ask for a round of cards before nightfall? My guess is that it was curiosity and the need to show off like a peacock after his long time in prison. But perhaps Rocco had heard rumours of a new grape Antonio's brother had created: a wondrous new wine, a wine so powerful it produced visions equal to Morgan le Fay and could seduce men into believing they lived in a magical kingdom. (It was also rumoured that Sebastiano was somehow in league with the sorceress. She was, after all, immortal.) And perhaps Rocco understood, like Antonio, that such a wine was priceless and could make him and his associates rich.

The events that followed are smudged, like a grease stain on a suit lapel, or blurred like a photo snapped when the camera suddenly moves just as the shutter is pressed. Were they arguing about who owed the next round of wine? Or was it merely a bad hand of cards—in other words, bad luck, which is just another form of fate finding its way in the world. In any event, fear ran swift and cold like a mountain stream through the hearts of all present that day, and no one came forward to say what they saw or knew.

What is clear is that after a few hands of Scopa, Antonio lunged and stabbed Rocco just below his shoulder, tearing the beautiful, new white shirt. Was it self-defense? Antonio struck first, reaching across the table before Rocco could pull out the knife hidden inside his right sock. And who was cheating whom? Uncertainty formed part of the fog and the blur and the slur from wine, a few said.

We do know that Pepe, terrified, ran into the café. Rocco's cousin picked up a chair and threw it at Antonio. He missed. Antonio grabbed Angelo by the neck and brought his head down against his knee and then, in disgust, kicked him.

The other card players watched in stunned silence.

The local authorities were called but lost interest after three days. The sly, calculating, and wilfully blind eye of a few Calabrian peasants didn't help matters. By that time Antonio was hiding in a barn outside of Bologna, where a cousin worked. The official search for evidence dragged on for months.

Truth and justice were pursued elsewhere. A secret brigand trial was convened and Carmine Maldenti was presented with a problem not unlike the Gordian knot a sailor must untie before he can board the last life raft. The brother of his son-in-law had stabbed the son of his most senior brigand. Though he cared little for Rocco Lupino and his drinking and bragging, he could ignore the calls for retribution for only so long. The fact that Carmine Maldenti's daughter was married to Antonio's brother is what had spared the Filo family from immediate reprisal by the Lupino family. It was not a question of guilt or innocence; he knew it was impossible to establish with any confidence how the fight had started and why. The events of that fateful evening were layered with accusations and counter-accusations, and the villagers, of course, remained silent. It all came down to a question of respect and honour, especially for the Lupino family who had a stabbed son, and therefore demanded vengeance.

Brigand justice was swift. The Filo family was to pay the Lupino family a seemingly impossible large fine, and to apologize for the suffering caused. It was agreed that Rocco would stay away from Antonio and his family. The Lupinos, for their part, were to accept the apology—and the money and produce—and to promise they would not seek revenge. On the surface it seemed like an equitable and fair judgment, although Antonio insisted it was Rocco who had insulted the family honour by suddenly blurting out his desire to kiss Rosalina's breasts. (Privately, Antonio guessed the real cause: Sebastiano's wine.)

Fearing Antonio would never be completely forgiven, his mother decided to send him packing to America. There he could work and help pay the family debt. She was certain that cards or his brother's wine or young girls were going to be the death of him, so she sent Sebastiano to keep an eye on his wilder, younger brother.

In early July 1914, the Filo brothers set sail from for America. In one of his trunks, Antonio had secretly hidden seventeen well-wrapped bottles of Sebastiano's wine.

That summer, Signora Filo, like the councils of state across Europe. twitched with anxiety and foreboding.

1972

It was April and the long siege of winter was retreating. The battle had wavered back and forth: the forces of sunshine and warm air winning one day, the forces of snow and cold wind striking back on another. The river had thawed along its banks, and here and there open stretches of dark water appeared, fringed with thin ice. Lucia's news stunned me. At first I stayed calm and asked her if she was sure. She nodded and said she was. She looked past me, her grey-blue eyes sad and weary for the first time ever. I couldn't bear to look at her directly; I stared instead at my black coffee and asked her again. She nodded; the visit to the doctor a week earlier had confirmed what she was sure she already knew. She then told me she didn't want the baby. I reached for her hand and she burst into tears. I looked around the restaurant to see if anyone was watching, thinking it must appear to be a lovers' quarrel. The guy flipping hash browns and a hamburger nip glanced over at us and then went back to working the greasy grill. Later, in the car, she repeated her story about her relationship with Hughie. Angry and shocked, I tried to rise above my feelings of hurt and betrayal. She needed my help. But the words How? Why? kept ricocheting inside my head.

—Oh it's so complicated, I don't know how to explain, she repeated over and over. She stared out the window, ignoring my rage and hurt. She was busy coping with her own feelings, and sat cold and remote from me, a blank look on her face

—I shouldn't have told you. But you are the only person who can help me right now.

She asked me not to do or say anything crazy, and to stay calm. She said she'd take care of everything—parents, appointments, the clinic. She just needed money to get herself to Vancouver. I asked her why, again, and she refused to answer.

I didn't know what to do or think. For the next few days my moods pitched between hurt and dark anger. I took long drives down Portage Avenue, out past St. James and the row after row of tidy apartment blocks, strip malls and shops. This stretch of Portage Avenue looked bland and meaningless; a monument to someone's aseptic of idea of order and cleanliness. As always, I was trying to escape. One day I skipped school and spent the afternoon downtown in the Paddlewheel Restaurant at the Bay, drinking coffee and smoking cigarettes, unable to focus on anything, hoping to run into Hughie. He was the only one I knew who had any real money.

By the time I tracked him down, Lucia had already left for a women's health clinic in Vancouver. I thought her capacity for deceit was breathtaking. I burned with resentment.

~~~

The wine was unpredictable. It inspired some men to feel sentimental and full of brotherly love, wanting to embrace family and friends. Others felt the urge to make passionate love to the first woman they saw in the bar or on the street. Some were turned into hopeless dreamers, and sat perfectly still in front of their glass, grinning, lost in their own marvellous thoughts and vacantly watching tobacco smoke swirl into erotic shapes. Yet others turned into impatient and defiant bulls, the blood coursing through their body fast and furious. The wine made them feel confident, proud, and invincible. They slapped the table and cried out for more, once the bottle was empty. As for the women, well, they were not permitted to bring the hybrid Greco Nero wine to their lips. In fact, no one fully understood the wine's power (except for Antonio), although stories about its effects had spread throughout the small villages near Cosoleto, where Antonio had sold the wine in the markets before he and Sebastiano banished themselves into exile. Those in the fishing villages along the western coast believed the wine's effects were caused by Morgan le Fay. The inland villagers believed it was the mysterious effect of a full moon on a fermenting wine barrel.

Hughie had also figured out the wine's power. He had no idea what caused its effects, nor did he care. All he cared about was keeping up with demand. The day that I discovered that the tap on the wine barrel was locked (perhaps my father having suspicions that someone was stealing his wine), I had grabbed a few blue-black bottles with odd-shaped corks to fill Hughie's order. They were in the far back corner of the pantry, covered with thin silver threads woven by a long-dead spider, and I thought my father would never notice them gone.

News of the wine spread on the street. Hughie became everyone's favourite Sunday bootlegger.

~~~

Hughie wanted to meet behind the Cornish library. I had told him I was surprised he knew about Lucia and me and the patio tucked away in the bend of the river.

—Where? You're kidding, right? What did you two do in winter? Ha ha.

—Fuck you.

A wave of sexual jealousy rose up as he taunted me.

The path towards the riverbank was slippery. Snow and mud and leaves clung to my boots. Bare, thin red branches snapped back, offended. I had arrived before Hughie, and walked back and forth on the dock, scraping chunks of mud from my boots. The smeared clumps of muck made the wet planks even more slippery. I stopped at the end of the dock and looked out across the river towards the silver dome of St. Anne's school for girls. The hiss of car tires and the dull echo from engines reverberated under the Maryland Bridge.

The river was swollen. The dock had been pushed higher against the riverbank and bumped against the half-thawed ice. I looked down at a large, jagged hole surrounded by thin ice. Under it, the water ran black and fast. An ice jam further out made the river look wild and desolate, more like a frozen parcel of Antarctica than a windswept prairie river.

Daylight was fading fast, and I was getting colder by the minute. I turned when I heard him coming through the bush, and saw right away there was something not right about him. His eyes were set with an intensity I had not seen before, and I could make out a strange grin on his face. I asked him if he was stoned and he laughed.

I shouted at him for being such a two-faced bastard and for fucking Lucia behind my back. He laughed again. What did you expect, he replied? What do you want? It was then I told him that Lucia was getting an abortion. He stopped laughing and stepped closer, lunging at me and throwing a fist at the same time.

What happened next unfolded fast and incoherent. I remember it as a series of black-and-white stills, vague and incomplete, mixed with feelings of panic, fear, and pain. We gripped each other's coats, and like scrappy hockey players, struggled in a weird dance. I slipped on a patch of smeared mud and we both veered sharply to the side, still holding onto each other, each of us trying to keep our balance. We were breathing hard; his breath smelt of wine.

I decided to slam down on his arms and then push him hard away from me. My sudden gesture caught him off guard. He lost his hold on me and fell back, but not before managing to let fly a punch just above my ear. There was a flash of white light before everything went black.

What I remember next was lying on my back on the dock and wondering why Hughie wasn't punching and kicking me. My head throbbed and I was still breathing hard. I managed to roll over and get up on my hands and knees. I touched the side of my head and felt the sticky texture of blood in my hair. I heard splashing sounds and looked up to see where they were coming from. Hughie was flailing in the icy water, desperately trying to kick himself forward to reach the dock. I tried to stand but couldn't, the pain in my head loud and fierce. I slowly crawled towards him and our eyes met. We said nothing. I could see the fear and panic in his eyes. He reached out again, and in a sudden burst of energy, grunting like a wild animal, he thrust his arms towards me. A few ice-cold drops splashed onto my face. The brass knuckles on one of his outstretched hands flashed briefly in the remaining light. I reached for him but fell short. Pausing for a moment to adjust my kneeling position on the dock, I reached out again. Then he stopped moving and went under, and this time did not return. It was as if his leaving was not a matter of great importance to anyone. I fell back onto the dock—exhausted, my head and ears ringing—and howled with rage at the evening sky.

1914

After nineteen days—four on the Mediterranean Sea and the remaining fifteen on the Atlantic Ocean—the Filo brothers arrived safe, but not necessarily sound, in New York Harbor on Monday, August 9th, six days after Britain declared war against Germany

After spending ten days sequestered on an island that resembled a prison, and another thirty days on the hot humid streets of the Lower East Side, Sebastiano longed to return home. He'd had enough of boiled potatoes and sweet white bread smudged with tomato, even though Antonio had discovered a kind Neapolitan woman who made a sauce rich with the nostalgic flavours and dreamy scents of Southern Italy in a kitchen at the back of a small six-table restaurant off Canal Street where they now ate once a week. The outbreak of the European War, otherwise known as the Great War, prevented a hasty return to the sunshine, fresh air, and cold, clean mountain water of Cosoleto. There was nothing to do but to stick to his original plan: work, save money, and return to Rosalina as quickly as possible.

Antonio, on the other hand, found himself intoxicated with America. There was nothing he did not embrace. The meat in the butcher shop was thicker, the potatoes bigger and tastier, the apples redder and sweeter, the tomatoes more plump and firmer, and the dizzying variety and abundance of women made his head spin with desire. It was as if he had drunk from a deep and refreshing well. His nerves tingled with excitement each morning—despite the squalor, the loud incessant noises, and the moisture-stained walls of their shabby, cramped apartment where they ate their suppers sitting at opposite ends of the bed. For Antonio, New York was a garden of earthly delights, and he regretted his inability to afford a new wardrobe. How could he be expected to make an impression on the women of America without a brand-new suit, a freshly starched collar, a firm crisp hat, and patent leather shoes?

It seemed to Antonio that he had not lived until his arrival on the animated streets of New York, bursting with people, sound, colour, and movement. This was not exile; it was deliverance from the old traditions of a church and honour-bound society. The New World was where life lived.

And there were Italians everywhere—building, sewing, cooking, washing, pouring, fixing, sweeping, lifting, and shovelling, their strong hands and bent backs in constant motion all over the Lower East Side and up and down Mulberry Street. The odd few had learned enough English to buy and sell fruits and vegetables. Fewer were those who had learned to use a fountain pen. Then there were the idle aristocrats who never worked, but were always well turned out. They cared little for the written word, although they were known to choose their words carefully. They wore fresh white shirts, polished black shoes, tailored jackets and coats, hats with soft round curves, and were always clean-shaven. These men were involved in *bizinees*. The immigrant Italians understood their work all too well.

You can see where all this is headed.

Letters arrived, addressed To Whom It May Concern: the black inked script regular and dense, the space between each word measured, the *o*'s round and firm, the *t*'s and *i*'s crossed and dotted, the *j*'s and *u*'s properly curved and balanced, the *y*'s coy and suggestive. The handwriting was not that of some semi-literate peasant but rather a well-schooled official, perhaps a lawyer asking, ahem, of the whereabouts of a certain Antonio Filo and his brother Sebastiano, pointedly detailing an outstanding debt to a certain Lupino family. The nib, catching the light as it moved across the white page slow and careful like a well-balanced sewing needle, had connected the letters that made words, and words placed in the right order became thoughts and for a moment gave the illusion the world could be made permanent by holding it still in a sentence between the narrow white spaces.

The written word brought cold detached reality to Antonio and Sebastiano, and turned their minds to the accumulated gestures and events of Calabrian village life and unforgiving, traditional rural customs.

Their mother's foresight had proved correct: the Lupino family would not forget the disrespect done to their son by Antonio Filo.

April 1972

I staggered back up the path towards the library, barely able to see where I was going, guided only by the glow of streetlamps. It was dark and cold, and my head ached. I could feel warm blood oozing on my temple. My mind was a complete blank, leaving me unable to produce a single organized thought.

I sat on the library steps, trying to catch my breath and to think about what I should do next, when I spotted a familiar-looking bottle. Someone had carefully propped it up against a large elm tree, between the sidewalk and the street. I remembered looking at similar bottles in my father's wine cellar when I was a child, and thinking how they were unlike any other bottles in his collection. I went over and picked it up. Sure enough, there was the distinct concaved bottom, engraved with the date 1905 and the words *Reggio di Calabria, Italia.* There was no mistaking it; this was one of my father's special wine bottles. Inside was a scrolled piece of paper. I shook it to get the note out. A few dark purple drops of wine, like blood, fell onto my palm. The note was barely legible, written in small scratchy words: *I guess I didn't have to beat you so bad. Ha Ha Ha. Your pal Hughie.*

The unexpected, pitiful irony of Hughie's note made me gasp. I smashed the bottle against the library's brick wall and burst into tears. I pulled myself together long enough to pick up the larger shards and walk to the centre of the Maryland Bridge. I dropped them into the river, one by one, and then walked the half block to Emergency at the Misercordia Hospital. I sat in the waiting room, hoping Hughie's wild punch wouldn't require stitches and trying to stem the steady panic rising inside me. He was gone. What was I going to do, I asked myself over and over. And was the baby Hughie's or mine? I felt scared, betrayed, humiliated. I had wanted it out with Hughie, to get to the truth. His bullshit had sickened me. Now he was gone; he'd slipped away right in front of me. Was it my fault? I wasn't sure.

The wine's ancient curse was the only truth I knew.

January 1919

This was the century of everyone leaving—leaving for the promise of something better; leaving for love; leaving a dead past and a closed future; leaving war. Fear was packed at the bottom of old wooden trunks lined with white linen, vague promises at the top, gold jewellery and a few lira hidden in the lining of jackets, dresses, even underwear. They crossed the wine-dark sea and arrived in the New World: from the very beginning, Europe's safety valve.

Sebastiano and Antonio were on the move—this time to Buffalo—to escape the long vengeful arm of the Lupino family. The letters with the beautiful script had made it clear that, should compensation not be immediately forthcoming, then perhaps the convenient death of Antonio (and perhaps even Sebastiano) could be arranged. But after their arrival in Buffalo, Antonio's cards and Sebastiano's wine again disrupted their exiled life. Sebastiano, knowing full well his brother could not be trusted, took what Antonio claimed to be all the remaining bottles of wine. They fled in opposite directions: Sebastiano to Winnipeg, the largest and coldest Canadian city west of Buffalo, and Antonio to South America to locate a friend who had written to him about the beauty, the easy money, and the late night gambling cafés of Buenos Aires. Antonio carefully wrapped in newspapers and cloth the wine bottles he had withheld from Sebastiano, and placed them in the centre of his wooden trunk. It was 1919, and they had agreed on the fly to meet back in Italy by year's end. There were no tears; only smiles that, once again, they had managed to escape the unpredictable effects of Sebastiano's wine.

~~~

Sebastiano didn't know it, but when he disembarked like a slapstick vaudeville actor at the CPR station on the corner of Logan and Main, Winnipeg was an angry city. Nor did he know that thousands of workers in Winnipeg were about to make history. Who could have predicted that in six months the Winnipeg General Strike would shock and surprise the entire North American continent?

Sebastiano quickly released his grip from the frozen steel handle of the train car. It was so cold, he felt he had burned his hand. He stumbled onto the platform, his cardboard suitcase pulled to his chest. Still bent at the waist, he lumbered towards a crowd of people. To avoid them, he veered away, still in full flight, but not before slipping on a piece of ice and falling, face first, on top of his suitcase—the whole scene a fast-moving but clumsy visual joke from a silent movie.

So much for his plan of discreetly slipping into the city, finding work, and then quietly slipping back to Southern Italy—preferably with a plump pack of Canadian dollars sewn into the lining of his jacket. The question remained of what to do about the Lupino family and the letters they had sent. He felt certain that, on his return, they could be bought with Canadian and American dollars.

Sebastiano's fall caught the attention of the watchful eyes of Signora Rapdi, who had managed the Gents' and Ladies' private dining rooms at the Mariaggi Hotel ever since Frank Mariaggi, the hotel's original owner, returned to Sardinia in 1908. She was at the station to meet her cousin's boy, and instead she was laughing, like everyone else, at the bumbling foreign traveller who had just fallen off the train.

—*Mai che e quello povero idiota*, who is that poor idiot? she thought. Her question was soon answered. Even though she was one railcar away, she could hear Sebastiano swearing and muttering. *Ah, e Italiano.* She decided to investigate.

Her cousin's son was nowhere to be seen or found, and she needed a new dish washer, fast. Why not hire this fallen Italian, instead of one those lazy, vodka-drinking and onion-eating (and -smelling) Ukrainians, or one of those ill-mannered English-speaking soldiers with *una fronte brutto*, ugly face?

At a glance, she knew she was dealing with a desperate man. The frayed cuffs of his winter coat and the cheap cardboard case betrayed him. Sprawled out on the platform, he looked confused, naturally, and when no one came to greet him or help or comfort him after his journey, she knew he was an orphan. Perfect: he will make a loyal and moldable employee, she thought. She led him out of the station, like a fisherman with the catch of the day.

Sebastiano, sore and confused, accepted her terms. She was a god-sent piece of luck, he thought, when right there on the spot she offered him a job and a room. She spoke Italian with a rolling, harsh Sicilian accent, but she was not bad looking. Guessing his thoughts, she warned him she was married. He told her not to worry: he had a wife back in Italy.

He started work the next day. When not washing dishes in the kitchen, he swept the halls and helped stock wine and beer in the Grotto Room, the private dining room downstairs built to resemble a sea cave in Sardinia. And every morning he removed the piles of turds left in front of the hotel after horse-drawn carriages delivered wealthy guests from the CPR station, or guests arrived to dine after an evening performance at the new Walker Theater. He was paid twenty cents a day.

The kitchen at the Mariaggi Hotel at mealtimes resembled a torpedoed ship. There were shouts from waiters to cooks, and cooks to waiters. The waiters, pushing past the swinging doors with silver-lidded trays of food, sometimes collided, and a roasted chicken or buttered potatoes would flip onto the sawdust floor. The chicken would be discreetly picked up and dipped in hot water; the potatoes dusted off and sent out again. Fuck the rich, was the general attitude in the kitchen. Rebellion was in the air. It was the only time the waiters respected the cooks.

Sebastiano's place in the kitchen was at the back, beside one of the two heavy cast-iron stoves where he boiled water to clean the dishes. All day long, heat from the hotplates and stoves came in waves. Sweat dripped off his brow and his face turned bright red. More often than not, the chef was impatient for clean plates or a pan, and would holler at him.

—Hurry up, you lazy dago! Your mother loves you, your girlfriend might like you, but I hate you! Sebastiano didn't understand a word, but he fantasized about beating the chef with one of the long wooden spoons used to stir the black-bottomed pots the vegetables and potatoes were boiled in.

Sebastiano shared a small room with the hotel's doorman, a broken war veteran who, like many returned veterans of the Great War, was always angry. The man tried to explain his feelings of betrayal, the suffering of those in the trenches, how so many back home had profited from the war, how the returning soldiers deserved better—but he soon realized it was pointless: the stupid wop didn't understand a word.

It was not until April—when he had finally learned some English—that Sebastiano fully understood what the cook and the doorman had been saying. It was also around this time that the Building Trades & Metal Workers understood that their call for better wages and working conditions were being ignored. The mood of the workers' committee simmered, like the pots of water on the stove at the Mariaggi Hotel.

And while the Building Trades & Metal Workers visualized a strike and the doorman his next drink, Sebastiano visualized a triumphant return home (after giving the cook a sound beating).

April 1972

I left the hospital the next morning around six, just as light began to climb like a vine up the bare trees. No damage; just a throbbing headache and a cut the size of a dime over my right ear. Earlier I had phoned my Aunt Rosa and told her I was sleeping over at a friend's house, and not to worry. She accepted my explanation without too much fuss. I was surprised.

—Michael, you are seventeen now and almost a man. Would you tell your mother this excuse?

—Zia, I'm in Transcona with a friend. It's a long drive back.

—You better not come home with a problem, Michael. If you are an honourable boy, you won't be up to any funny business. I don't want to be blamed for any trouble you cause your family. Think of your poor mother in Italy, hoping to find a cure for her sickness. The doctors here know nothing! Don't make things worse.

—I always think of my mother.

—I know you do, Michael. You are a good boy. See you tomorrow. And don't sleep in too late. I'll tell your uncle you went to the library early. I hope you are not lying, for the sake of both of us.

Two weeks earlier, my mother had demanded that my father take her to Italy so she could see a specialist she'd heard about from a relative. The needle Dr. Albo had given her and the expensive pills he'd prescribed had done nothing but make her vomit and feel worse. She told my father that if he didn't take her to see this doctor, her death would be on his conscience. Overnight, our house had gone into a tailspin, and I had landed at my aunt and uncle's place on Furby Street, awaiting my parents' return.

I walked down Sherbrook to Westminster and turned right towards Broadway. Small mounds of snow freckled with dirt clung to the sidewalk and the grass lay soggy under thin windowpanes of ice. The huge green-coppered cupola of the Legislative Building struck a grand pose. On top, the Golden Boy faced north, cradling a sheath of wheat in his left arm and holding up a torch in his right hand, beckoning one and all northward, towards a better future. Shallow white-and-gold light spilled over the eastern horizon as the city came to life. Buses were packed with people on their way to work and the streets filled with morning rush-hour traffic. I felt like a fugitive amongst the earnest civic activity all around me.

I cut across the Legislative grounds and headed towards Las Vegas Amusement Centre, a billiard hall and pinball joint much like the Diamond on Notre Dame, only with bigger pool tables and more of them. It was a place for serious players, and a place to make small drug deals and sell hot clothes and electronics pinched from downtown stores, especially the Bay across the street. Hughie had spent a lot of time there. I needed to talk to Nicola.

Nicola used to rent a room on the third floor of my parents' house on Langside Street when he first came to Canada. He had worked at a bunch of bad-paying jobs and lived on cheap pasta and sardine sandwiches before he took over Las Vegas Amusements from the owner, a parishioner of Holy Rosary Church. On Sunday afternoons, Nicola smoked his way through half a dozen Cameo Menthols and lectured me on the parallels between ancient Roman history and current American politics. Like most self-educated men, he admired his own intellect and was more or less a one-trick pony. Roman history, period. Still, I had liked talking to him—he was in his late twenties and his youthful energy was part of the appeal—and we continued to be friends after he moved out of our house. I thought maybe Nicola could help me figure out what to do. Tell me what the cops knew, or thought they knew, about Hughie (before he ended up in the river) and my Dad's wine.

The pool hall was closed until nine, so I continued to the Salisbury House, passing Eaton's Warehouse where Hughie and I used to spend Saturday afternoons before Christmastime admiring and desiring the latest expensive toys. I sat down on a red vinyl-topped stool at the counter and ordered coffee and a doughnut. My head still ached from the hit I took the night before; my stomach was empty and queasy.

When I went back to Las Vegas, four guys were playing pool near the back exit. An open duffle bag lay across two chairs next to them, easy to grab if they got a signal from Nicola and needed to get away in a hurry. They glanced over, and then returned to their game. Nicola was leaning on his elbow on the counter, sipping an espresso and smoking.

Against the wall behind him, pool cues of various sizes were lined up in rows. He was surprised to see me.

—Hey Michael, no school today? How you gonna to win a scholarship if you start hanging out here?

I offered a fake smile. —You need time off, Nicola. Espresso, please.

—I hear your parents went back to Italy all of a sudden. Everything okay? Man, you look beaten up.

I touched my head. It was pounding. At the hospital a nurse had washed off my hair and cleaned the cut Hughie gave me, but the 222 tablets she'd given me were not helping.

—Everything's fine. Just tired and worried, I guess. I was up late studying. Thought I'd take the day off and hang out with Hughie. Have you seen him?

—That guy is an asshole, Michael. Stay away from him. He's nothing but bad news. Why would a nice boy like you want to hang around with a bastard like him?

—What time does he show up?

—Usually around one. But I'm telling you, Michael, stay away from him. The Bay security was in here looking for him. So were the cops. Don't take anything from him and don't buy whatever he's selling. Nicola narrowed his eyes and lowered his voice. I hear he's got his hands on some crazy wine.

I nodded and downed the espresso in two quick gulps. Thanks. If you see him, tell him I was looking for him.

I went up the stairs and out the door, returning to the bright moral sunshine of a new spring day. I walked to the corner and crossed Portage Avenue to catch the bus. My head now throbbed with a dull, consistent pain. I was afraid, and trying to stop myself from crying. My fear mixed with foreboding. The right thing to do was to go to the police and explain everything. Tell them why Hughie and I had met up on the dock. Tell them about our childhood friendship. Tell them about Lucia, her plans for an abortion, her mad father, my depressed mother, the afternoon in the grain elevator, the bus rides, the secret library visits, the 1783 earthquake, the ancient potent wine hidden in our basement by my father…

But I was a coward.

The shame haunts me.

1919

On the first of May 1919, after months of labour negotiations, the building workers of Winnipeg went on strike for better wages. The following day the metalworkers also went on strike when the employers of the main metalwork factories refused to negotiate with their union. Anger, quiet and deep, began to spread through the city as workers everywhere watched and waited. Some members of the Winnipeg Trades and Labour Council advocated patience and calm; other council members were stunned by the arrogance of the owners and employers. If the employers again refused to meet with the labour leaders, there seemed no option but to call for a general strike. But what if the call went unheeded? What then? How were workers supposed to feed their families if no one came to their support? And it was important that violence and vandalism be avoided at all costs: no sense giving the authorities ammunition to continue ignoring the unions and their demand to be recognized as the legitimate voice of the workers.

As for the business owners, they began plotting how to get rid of the striking workers. Spies in the rank and file reported back to the owners that support for the strike was, in their words, a mile wide but an inch deep, and in a few days the strike would collapse. The employers argued there were many who were willing to replace the strikers and work for twenty-five cents a day, or less. Half the striking workers barely spoke English; how dare such an uneducated rabble make demands and try to undermine British values, not to mention peace, order, and good government. What woolliness had inspired the Labour Council? How was it possible that sensible, born-and-bred Englishmen could support and lead such a mob? Mind, only a year ago a group of crazed Bolsheviks did mange to overthrow the Russian Czar. Whatever had happened to the rule of law?

In this atmosphere Signora Rapdi advised Sebastiano to *fa i cazzi tuoi*, mind your own business, and ignore the speeches and gatherings. She had heard about one skirmish in a small city park on the edge of the city limits off Logan Avenue. She knew there was idle talk of a general strike, just like a few years before when workers in the city had complained about low wages and long hours. Such is life, she thought.

—You are here to make money for your family, right? So work, and you make your money. Ignore these malcontents. Why should you care about them? Do they care about you, a poor Italian in this frozen country? *L'ingles, vi lascere moiré come un cane,* the English would let you die like a dog.

In Sebastiano's mind, the signora's advice made perfect sense. It was only a question of time before he and his brother would triumphantly return back to Italy with money to quietly buy more land, to put food on the table. Yes, there was still the problem of the unhealed respect wound to the Lupino family, but surely between them, he and Antonio would have enough money to smooth over any residual ill-will that he imagined brooded within their ranks and stalked the Lupino family like a wounded wolf.

Sebastiano followed Signora Rapdi's advice. He didn't flinch from his daily tasks and kept up the routines established since his first days at the hotel. He awoke every morning at five, splashed his face with cold water, and dressed. He took the back stairs to the kitchen to light the stoves before the cooks arrived at five-thirty to prepare breakfast for the hotel guests. (Breakfast was served punctually at seven every day except Sunday.) He would heat a small kettle and return with it to his room, pour the hot water into a chipped metal basin, and carefully but quickly shave in front of the spotted mirror above the washstand. Back in the kitchen he would eat a thick slab of bread with butter, and gulp down a cup of black coffee just as the cook and two assistants arrived after another night of drinking, their eyes narrow and faces red and shiny as if glazed with melted sugar. Between reporting to Signora Rapdi for any additional tasks, he swept the front entrance, unloaded the laundry carts, heated up two tubs of water for washing the breakfast dishes, and then was off to shovel coal, chop wood, wax the stairs, polish the brass railings, clean windows, scrub the men's baths, carry out loads of trash, and so on. This he did from six in the morning until nine in the evening, six days a week, fifteen hours a day.

But one morning Sebastiano sensed something was wrong, or at the very least, different from what he had been accustomed to the last several months. His roommate was not in his bed, snoring. Of course, maybe he hadn't returned from his night out to one of the saloons on Main Street. In the kitchen, there was no cook, and only one of the assistants had shown up.

He went out to look around. McDermot Street was quiet and still, as it always was at that time of day. It was a cool morning; the sun a thin, gold disc behind fat grey-and-white clouds. In the distance he heard the familiar clang of a street-car coming down Main Street. It was the proverbial calm before the storm.

At eleven o'clock, the general strike went into effect. Office workers, bricklayers, carpenters, plumbers, telegraph and telephone operators, factory workers, retail store clerks, waiters and waitresses, bakery and candy workers—basically all of Winnipeg's working population went on strike in support of the Building and Metal Trade Councils. Arthur and Albert Streets around the Mariaggi Hotel began to fill with men and women. The 'Hello Girls' from the telephone exchange walked over from the corner of King Street and milled about freely with the city's office workers. At the corner of William and Main, beside City Hall, a huge crowd gathered.

Signora Rapdi prided herself on understanding her adopted city, but the general strike had caught her by complete surprise. The entire staff of the hotel had walked out and joined the strikers. There was no one left to clean, cook, serve, or receive patrons, not that any were arriving now that the strike was on.

The strike had another effect. It unexpectedly threw Sebastiano and Signora Rapdi closer together that first long day—and then the next and the next. The trains did not stop in the city for long and the out-of-town guests fled in a hurry. When the last guest finally left, Signora Rapdi, exhausted, closed the hotel. That evening, she cooked a simple dinner of ham and eggs for the two of them. Sebastiano went to his room and returned with a bottle of his wine from Italy.

—It's a beautiful wine, Signora. I made it myself, in Italy. I have been saving it for a special occasion. Have some. It will give you energy.

—Oh, Sebastiano, you are the only one who stayed at my side—not like the rest of those beasts. You are so kind. *Salute.*

The wine coursed through their veins and a thousand little explosions rippled through their bodies after each sip. Perhaps Signora Rapdi had been secretly longing for a private moment since the day she first saw Sebastiano at the train station. His buffo entrance had made her laugh. It had been ages since she had felt the warmth of her long-gone husband against her skin. Perhaps the secret, seductive siren call of desire and the laughter and his wine mixed in a forgotten cauldron inside her heart and stirred up ignored feelings, feelings she had buried and mistrusted for years.

It was the vagaries of history and the unintended consequences of a general strike that brought them together—on the one hand, a wandering lone Calabrian contadino who like a latter-day Oedipus kept trying to escape his origins and fate only to find himself one May evening in a Winnipeg hotel with a beautiful woman; on the other, a hard-nosed and fatigued Sicilian hotel manager whose passion was ignited by an ancient hybrid wine.

Sebastiano marvelled at the layers and layers of undergarments Signora Rapdi wore. As each one came off with a time-consuming struggle (there were so many buttons and clasps!), the heady odour of sweat and garlic filled the air. He kissed her neck; it was warm and soft and perfumed. She moaned. She held his head in her hands and kissed his forehead, then pushed it down towards her concealed, curved plum until he caught her meaning and travelled alone. The musky earthy scent he found there (reminiscent of freshly picked forest mushrooms, he recalled later on board the ship to Italy while staring out at the vast endless grey sea and the distant horizon glowing pink and magenta), the salty pleasure, and her enthusiastic muscular desire he would remember for the rest of his life.

Signora Rapdi, for her part, could not forget what she saw when she turned sideways to avoid his gaze as he entered her. On the floor, beside his right shoe and a heap of crumpled petticoats, a pair of round, pouty lips sprouted from the top of the blue-black wine bottle from which they had been drinking. The lips opened and closed, like the mouth of a slowly feeding goldfish, and then were gone. She moaned like a woman tied to the moon. Shortly after, she sang a song she thought she had long forgotten.

And thus the wine, again the wine, sent Sebastiano packing, this time back to Italy. Winnipeg was forever etched in his gentle soul as a place of cold refuge and brief ill-timed pleasure.

It is a cool, fall night. Streetlamps glow a dull orange. I'm driving north on Route 90, past the suburban idle of River Heights on one side and the edge of Tuxedo on the other, heading towards the industrial wasteland of Winnipeg's North End. Not much on the road tonight except a few cars and slow-moving buses and semis that grunt, snort, and snarl down the highway heading for the perimeter. I've spent a restless evening trying to write this story. The dreary street scenes fit my taciturn mood.

I am no longer a young man. Guilt and shame still knock, but over the years I have put up a huge medieval gate to keep them out. What led up to Hughie's fall into the river? Whose baby was it? Why did I allow the silence between me and my mother to grow? She needed me and I had wanted to run away.

Now everything is forever.

July 1972

My father's urgent telegram arrived at my aunt and uncle's home on a Saturday morning some weeks after the incident on the dock. Lucia had not yet returned from the coast. A thunderstorm had swept through the city in a single blast of wind and rain. Large raindrops battered the window, streaked, and then dissolved into small blobs of water. An expression my mother used to say came to mind: *Il mondo non e lo stesso dopo che piove,* the world is not the same after it rains.

My aunt was crying in the kitchen. Events seemed to have found their own synergy and rhythm, and were steadily moving from bad to worse.

After a few frenzied phone calls, my Uncle Joe found an Italian travel agent who condescended to arrange my flight to Italy. Initially he told my uncle that, though he appreciated the situation was urgent, he was unable to book a flight until Monday. Furious, my uncle demanded he find a flight that very evening, adding that he would hold him responsible if my mother died before I arrived in Italy.

We drove to the airport in silence, except for my aunt reciting one Hail Mary after another under her breath. The streets were wet and shiny, and caught the light from headlights and streetlamps. It reminded me of a coffee-table book of Paris and London in the 1920s that I'd looked at with Lucia, showing rainy streets crowded with a bloom of umbrellas. I imagined living a different life in a different city inside a different self, far away from the confused drama of events unfolding around me. Even as my mother lay sick and perhaps dying on the other side of the world, I longed to escape. I felt ashamed.

I arrived, jet lagged, and was driven straight to the Riuniti Hospital in Reggio di Calabria by an older relative I'd never heard of. He'd picked me out of the small crowd gathered beside the luggage carousel and asked me if I was Michael Filo, son of Nino and Carmela. He seemed pleased he had found me so quickly. *I vostri vesti e nemeno fumi come un italiano del' paesi*, it's your clothes and you don't smoke like an Italian from Italy.

We barely spoke in the car. I was tired and he decided to leave me to my own thoughts. He dropped me off and said he would return with my father, who had gone home to rest.

My mother's room was on a small ward on the fourth floor. The white walls of the hallway were covered with black scuffmarks, as if a soccer game had been played in the corridor. The stuccoed ceiling was flaking and stained with brown watermarks. There were no nurses in sight.

She was propped up, staring at the wall. Both the room and the bed were small. There was barely enough space for the washstand and the dented standup cupboard where fresh linens, medicine, and patients' toiletries were kept locked up. (It seemed that stealing from the sick and the dying was not uncommon in the hospital.) I stood, uncertain, framed by the door entrance. She sensed my presence and turned and smiled. She told me to hurry and go pick up her wedding dress; she had washed and pressed my shirt and pants the day before but I needed to ask cousin Pino for a tie. She reminded me to polish my shoes.

—Ma, its your son Michael. How are you?

She ignored my question and continued to reminisce about her wedding day. Her grandfather had hired the accordionist and the cook from the nearby town of Sant'Eufemia d'Aspromonte, to season and roast a slaughtered pig and lamb on the eve before the wedding feast. The split carcasses, rubbed with oregano, rosemary, pepper, salt, and garlic, had been slowly roasted over charcoal, hours before the ceremony. A light breeze caught the scent of roasting meat and carried it up the road, across the small piazza and down the narrow village streets in abrupt, fragrant waves.

Tables for the guests were set up end-to-end beneath the shade of olive trees and a pergola. When there were not enough tables, long planks (and even an old door arrived, accompanied with great fanfare) were placed on top of wine barrels and covered with white cloth. Chairs arrived in twos and threes from every invited household. The olive leaves above the tables and chairs flashed grey and green in the bright June light.

My mother stopped for a moment to look around the room and then at me. I was familiar with how her wedding day had unfolded. It was a story she had told me many times before.

The tables filled quickly after the ceremony and eventually people were eating everywhere—on the balcony stairs overlooking the garden, against the trees, beside the tool shed. Everyone was shouting and laughing and twirling thick coils of pasta the size of a baby's fist.

The men poured homemade wine—the taste, flavour,

colour, the lunar hour and day the wine began fermenting, the quality of the wine barrels, water source, character and angle of the soil, the shape of the grape itself—were hotly debated, each man competing and trying to out-reason, out-shout, and out-bluff the other after each glass to prove his was the superior wine.

The conversation inevitably turned to the mysterious and limited wine made years before by the father of the groom. Someone said in a hushed tone that the wine was the reason the brother never returned from Argentina; the police had found his body stuffed in a trashcan on a side street in the Palermo district, the Italian immigrant ghetto of Buenos Aires, his throat slit. Wine had nothing to do with it, said another man. Antonio loved women, and it was his love of another man's woman that got him killed.

Another guest offered a different explanation: It was cards and the rough crowds he couldn't stop hanging around that made for his bad end. You know that they found the body around the corner from a late-night gambling bar.

—You are all wrong. It was the revenge of the Lupino family. Antonio was no fool.

—No, I say it was the curse of Morgan le Fay. Maybe even an old gypsy curse. *Il anticho proverbi dici*, just like the proverb says: A woman, wine, and a gypsy curse always lead to a bad end.

Round and round the comments went, and each time a new detail was added until someone finally said: Stop! Enough already. This is supposed to be a happy day. *Cambi il discorso*, change the subject, and drink to the happy, horny days of the bride and groom. The men laughed in one quick burst that sounded like applause.

The accordionist started up and people began to dance. Tambourines thudded and rattled and flashed in the sun. Family and friends wished the newlyweds well.

~~~

A nurse bustled into the room, her entrance pulling my mother out of her wedding reverie. She asked my mother how she was feeling ('Tired' was the response), checked her temperature, and then turned to me and asked if I was a relative.

—Ah, the son! What a good boy—*un bravo ragazzo*— you are, visiting your mother. So many, these days, do not come to the hospital. The smell of the sick and dying is nauseating to them.

—What 's wrong with her?

—No one has told you?

—I arrived from Canada this afternoon.

The nurse gave me a solemn look and waved for me to follow her out of the room.

—I thought your Italian sounded a bit strange. Listen… I'm sorry to tell you this: the tests say it's serious. Your mother has leukemia. I'm sorry; nothing can be done to change her situation.

~~~

My father and I took her home to Cosoleto. We arranged for a nurse to come by every two days to check up on her and for the local physician, old Dr. Scarcella, to visit. We argued over her care almost every day.

Nicola called from Canada to tell me, with regrets, that Hughie's body had been fished out of the Red River. The story was on page two of the Winnipeg Free Press and was also mentioned on the TV evening news. His army overcoat had snagged on a fallen tree near the Lockport Dam. He had been in the water for over two months, and his body was bloated and waterlogged, his features almost completely erased. An autopsy had found wine and drugs in his system, and in the wine traces of some kind of strange amphetamine. No signs of foul play: no bruises, wounds, or stab marks, although, oddly, he was wearing brass knuckles on one hand. Hughie had been a loner and not well liked, and since neither his family nor the cops missed him, there was not much of an investigation, although a few cops had shown up at the pool hall and asked some questions. While there, they'd busted a shoplifting gang, hoping for a lead to someone who wanted Hughie dead, but that line of reasoning had gone nowhere. The cops did ferret out some former girlfriends, the scrappy one with black fingernail polish and the bleached blonde, but each in her own way had said Hughie had been acting strange before he went missing. One of them thought she'd heard him say he was going to be a father, that it was time for him to start cleaning up his act, that he was going to settle down with a nice girl—but Hughie was always joking about changing his life. Besides, it was impossible to think of him as anything but a drug dealer and a thief.

Nicola concluded: Hughie killed himself, was the final verdict, Maybe something personal, maybe not. Maybe there was a girl somewhere who knew the reason, maybe not. He was a punk, a thief, and drug dealer, and there was no reason to care, one way or the other. The body had been in the water for so long, it was impossible to tell where and when he had gone in.

After Nicola's call, I took a long walk past the outskirts of the village and ended up looking down from the side of the road at overgrown bomb craters that had once been my grandfather's sloped vignetto. The worn edges of the craters were now covered with thin wild grass.

Further down the road was the graffiti-covered pillbox the Fascists had carved out of the mountainside in the thirties but had been used instead by retreating German soldiers during the invasion of Italy. The pillbox was at the centre of a fork in the road and sat above a deep ravine. Its position commanded the approach from the coastal road. The first wave of advancing British and American troops were unable to destroy the pillbox, and rather than waste time waiting to bring up artillery, they called for air strikes. The first bombs wildly missed their target: the little fortress was at an odd and impossible angle. The bombs destroyed instead most of the cultivated terrain below the road. But the bomb attacks did underline to the handful of defenders that their situation was hopeless, and they slipped away at nightfall. In the clear light of day, the advancing Allied troops walked up the road towards Cosoleto, past the smoldering black ruins of what was once Sebastiano's vignetto, and shrugged.

I looked at the craters. The hybrid vineyard and its grape had vanished with the bombs. Not that the vineyard had produced much by way of visionary wine since Sebastiano's ill-fated voyage across the Atlantic. When he returned to Southern Calabria in 1919, he more or less finally understood, thanks to the minnow kisses of Signora Rapdi and the heartfelt melody of her sighs, that the wine he produced in the fall of 1913 and that Antonio had sold and trafficked, was an extraordinary wine. But the vignetto was no longer the same one he'd left behind. The vines that were left still produced grapes, but something had happened to the sugar and overall chemistry so that the fruit looked more like overgrown peas than plump, dark globes. Yet the legend of the wine lived on for years to come, and many in the surrounding valleys themselves claimed to have produced the extraordinary powerful wine. Sebastiano cursed his fate.

I continued on down the road, the incessant sound of cicadas all around me. The grey-green leaves of olive trees on the terraced hills flashed in the sun. The afternoon was hot and still. Villagers in the surrounding settlements enjoyed afternoon siestas. The steady, determined whine of a Vespa climbing an incline on the winding road below, receded in the distance. The breeze picked up and caressed my face, the way Lucia's hand had traced the contours of my brow and cheek before she boarded the bus back to Athens, alone.

—It doesn't matter anymore, Michael. Forgive.

—You were sad for a long time.

—There is nothing to do or think. I can't explain who I was so long ago. Stop looking. Stop asking. I want to be free of the past. Move on, Michael. Happiness is overrated. Better to live a free life. Isn't that what we wanted?

I heard a splash followed by a loud, wet slap that echoed off the ancient stone walls. Someone was washing clothes in the grotto below the village fountain. Hughie's panicked face surfaced for a moment in my mind and then disappeared, just as quickly as it had under the cold, fast current of the Assiniboine River that April evening. In my mind's eye, I saw Carmela glance over her shoulder to watch Nino stare at the dark blue mountains.

My mother died a few weeks later, my father and I at her beside, numb with grief and disbelief. She left like everyone else, quietly and simply, never understanding why her life had formed the way it did, built one day at a time from rough-hewn blocks, and only half-assembled and in ruins by the time she left.

~~~

Lucia and Hughie's secret was forever my burden. His death was a cold, dark shadow between us; the arc of our lives transformed by his death. In Greece with Lucia, I'd been searching for the beginning of my past, hoping for a new beginning, praying that the sunburnt landscape, olive trees, and the sea would release me from unwelcome memories. Then came the countless unforeseen events and acts that would shape our identities and our fates in a way that was unpredictable and impossible to unravel.

The past was too much for her. The abortion had left her unfertile and grieving. Lucia had wanted forgiveness and some kind of comprehension or perspective, and to throw off the yoke of Hughie's death—something, it was clear to her, that was impossible. I had underestimated her remorse, and her anger and sadness at not being able to have children. Her wound lay under her skin, unarticulated and compressed; an unfinished and unsent letter written across the surface of her heart.

Grief, however, has its own sense of timing.

And when Lucia got on the bus, she never looked back.

All my life I have longed for something I cannot even name. Tonight I wait for the return of the white nothingness of another winter. The complex silence that comes after death is what remains, like the silence at the end of a story before one returns to the dream of life.

ACKNOWLEDGEMENTS

An excerpt from the novella – "Early, 1900's" – (pages 48-50) is to be published later this year in an anthology called *Italian-Canadians at the Table*, Guernica Press.

My thanks to Steve Snyder for his ceaseless enthusiasm and generosity before and after the writing.

Special thanks to Trish Loewn, mindful editor extraordinaire, although the nib did stay on.

A book is almost always a product of the countless gestures of handmaidens (male and female) to numerous to mention but frequently found in the vincity of Bar Italia. Each of you know who are and thank you.

ABOUT THE AUTHOR

Carmelo Militano is a Winnipeg poet and writer. He was born in the village of Cosoleto, province of Reggio di Calabria, Italy and immigrated to Canada at an early age with his parents.

He worked as a CBC Radio One journalist and broadcaster before returning to poetry. As a poet he is the winner of the 2004 F.G. Bressani award for poetry for his collection *Ariadne's Thread* (Olive Press, 2004). He has since published *The Minotaur's Keys* (Olive Press, 2006) a chapbook, collected poems *Feast Days* (Olive Press, 2010) and another chapbook Weather Reports (Olive Press, 2011) which was short-listed in 2012 for the Bressani poetry award.

His prose includes the travelogue and family memoir *The Fate of Olives* (Olive Press, 2006) short-listed twice in two different years. He writes literary essays and reviews and conducts interviews for a wide-range of publications across Canada and the USA. They include *Accent(i), CV2, Italian Canadiana, Northern Poetry Review, Pacific Rim Review of Books, Popmatters*, and *Prairie Fire*.

He reluctantly gave up chicken and hog farming for literature.